JUST IMAGINE . . .

Ramsey Campbell, whose specialty is writing books that chill the blood and make the flesh creep, that make you look carefully at the shadows behind your familiar armchair.

JUST IMAGINE . . .

What kind of story would scare *him*, what depths of terror lurk with these pages. Make yourself comfortable, settle down, turn on all the lights. Welcome to the banquet of fine frights.

Also by Ramsey Campbell
published by Tor Books

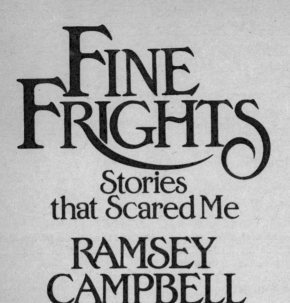

FINE FRIGHTS

Stories that Scared Me

RAMSEY CAMPBELL

TOR
HORROR

A TOM DOHERTY ASSOCIATES BOOK

for Peter Straub
and Stephen King
who deserve to be in this book

FINE FRIGHTS

A TOR Book
Published by Tom Doherty Associates, Inc.
49 West 24 Street
New York, NY 10010

ISBN: 0-812-51670-2   Can. ISBN: 0-812-51671-0

First edition: August 1988

Printed in the United States of America

0 9 8 7 6 5 4 3 2 1

Acknowledgments

Contents

Introduction

I've wanted to bring out this book for years—I suppose ever since I realized how many of my readers had never read some of my favorite horror stories. Part of the reason seems to be that a considerable number of readers have only recently discovered the field. I envy them their discovery of the great tradition of the horror story, to which I mean to introduce them here with stories such as "Thurnley Abbey" and "The Necromancer." I hope that specialists in the field will find themselves rewarded too, by the unjustly neglected work of Villy Sørensen and Thomas Ligotti, among others. Keeping in mind the numerous horror anthologies whose contents overlap, I've done my best to make sure that at least half of this book will be unfamiliar to any given reader.

It contains only a sampling of stories that scared me, of course, and of the authors whose work has done so. The tales of Dennis Etchison and Stephen King, for instance, are readily available in paperback; Peter Straub and Jim Herbert are novelists rather than tellers of short stories. All the same, I could compile a companion volume of material as unfamiliar as this one contains, and perhaps the sales of this one will justify my doing so. Tell your friends! Meanwhile, I should like to thank my editor Harriet McDougal and all the other good folk at Tor Books for bringing this book to you.

RAMSEY CAMPBELL
Merseyside, England

CHILD'S PLAY

by Villy Sørensen

Villy Sørensen is one of the most respected living Danish writers. He was born in 1929, and in 1953 he published his first book of short stories. Since then he has published essays and biographies (*Seneca: the Humanist at the Court of Nero* is available in English). The University of Nebraska Press will bring out a new collection of his tales in 1988 or 1989. In 1956 his first collection appeared in English as *Strange Stories*. The first story, "Child's Play," shocked me deeply when I read it, and it disturbs me still.

TWO BOYS WHO were brothers because they had the same parents had an uncle in common too, who had to have his leg taken off. This made their uncle such an object of interest in the boys' eyes that their parents decided they would have to be given a scientific explanation of the affair to put their minds at rest. Uncle had got a hole in his toe and a lot of animals had crawled in through the hole and right up his leg. These animals were so small that you couldn't even see them. Father called them bacteria and mother bacilli, so that the elder boy chose to call them bactilla and the younger batteries. These strange animals crawled in a red strip up uncle's leg, so

3

the leg had to be sawn off before they reached his body, for if they did that uncle would die. But now he had an artificial leg and was still alive and the leg was just as good as a real one. With this explanation the parents thought their children were content.

A little boy was running barefoot alongside a horse and cart. He was trying to find out how a horse has four legs and yet still manages to run. But he quite forgot how he himself should run and suddenly he got such a pain in his big toe that it seemed as if there was no other feeling in his whole body. He hopped about on one leg and said, "Ooh!" and screwed up his little face that would never get any bigger. He had stubbed his toe against a hard stone and a large drop of blood fell from it into the gutter . . . just as the two older boys came by.

"Ooh! Now he's got blood poisoning," said the smallest. "You must go and see a doctor."

"No! I don't want to."

"Perhaps you don't know it but you've made a hole in your big toe and a lot of animals will come in through it and crawl right up your leg."

The little boy looked at his big toe curiously.

"You're only making fun of me. I can't see any animals."

"No, you won't. They're so small you can't see them. They're called batteries."

"Bactilla," his elder brother corrected him

4

sagely. "If they reach your body you'll die. So you must have your leg taken off."

"I want to keep my leg. It's mine!" said the little boy and took hold of his leg with both hands.

"Do you want to die?"

"Yes," said the little boy. Like everyone else he had not tried dying, so he did not think of it as especially important.

"He doesn't know what dying means. He's silly. Don't you see, if you die you don't go on living."

"I don't care!"

"If you're not alive you can't eat any more or play any more."

"I don't care. I'm a horse!"

"But if you're dead you can't even be a horse "

"I'm not dead."

"You're silly. You will die if you don't have your leg taken off. Because you've got blood poisoning and the bactilla have already run up past your knee. You must go to the doctor and have your leg sawn off."

"I won't go to the doctor. He sticks things in you."

"The doctor is very clever," the younger brother began now. "He'll only saw your leg off so the batteries won't hurt you."

"Bactilla," said his big brother.

But by now the little boy, whose toe had

stopped bleeding, had quite lost his nerve. He opened his mouth so wide that he nearly swallowed his little head and began to howl loudly. The two big boys, who were, to be sure, only small in comparison with any bigger boy, began to feel sorry for him.

"Never mind," said the eldest, "we will do it. We'll take him home and saw off his leg. We can use my fretsaw."

"But . . . we can't do that."

"Of course we can. A thin leg like that's nothing after the tree trunk I sawed up as easy as anything the day before yesterday. What's your name?"

"Peter," the little boy said. He was crying so much he could hardly speak.

"Come along, then, Peter. You needn't go to the doctor. I'll saw your leg off for you."

"I want to have my leg," shouted the little boy. "I want your leg too, I'm a horse."

"But we'll let you keep it. And you'll get an artificial leg too, which is just as good as a real one, and then you'll have three. But we must hurry up, because the bactilla can run very quickly up a little leg like yours."

"But can I have my leg to keep?"

"Of course. You can take it home and play with it."

"I want to be a horse when I grow up," explained the little boy, going along trustingly

6

with the two brothers. "A horse can run as fast as anything."

The two big boys agreed with him and swelled with importance because they condescended to agree with him.

"We'll get our names in the papers," whispered the elder brother to the younger.

Luckily there was no one there when they got home, so they laid Peter ready on the kitchen table and the eldest boy went to look for his fretsaw. Peter was babbling away about how fast horses could run and did not suspect anything even when the little boy pulled off his trousers and his brother picked up the saw. But as soon as the teeth of the saw touched his leg he started kicking wildly and screaming that he wanted to go home. The boys found it quite impossible to make him see reason and there was nothing for it but to tie him down with the clothesline. He had surprising strength although he was so small and it was a terribly long time before they managed to tie the rope properly round his body and then round the table legs. But at last he was tied so that he could not move. He still shrieked so hysterically, though, that the elder brother could not make himself heard when he gave orders to the younger, and he had to stuff a handkerchief into the screaming mouth. He got his fingers bitten until they bled, but that did not bother him. He was a plucky boy.

He set the saw boldly into the leg, well above the knee. He was unpleasantly surprised at the amount of blood there was in such a little leg, but they agreed it must be an indication of how far advanced the blood poisoning was. It was high time it was seen to. He went on sawing and torn pieces of red flesh broke round the cut, which was not as straight as it should have been.

"Phew," he said. "It's strange stuff to saw in. You try."

The younger boy set to work, rather uncertainly because his brother had never allowed him to borrow the saw before. As he was not used to sawing he did not notice anything strange about it and said:

"It's fun sawing."

"You're not getting anywhere. Let me!"

The big boy took the saw again while his brother skipped delightedly up and down the bleeding floor. He was greatly taken aback when the other said:

"This is a silly leg . . . it won't come off."

"Let me try."

Without any argument the elder brother handed over his saw. The blood dripped on to the floor like rain and crept across it like a huge snake.

"We must get all this cleared up before mother comes home."

The younger brother stopped sawing and

looked at the other in surprise. He noticed he was sweating.

"But . . . won't he get blood poisoning?"

"You don't think I care about that. Father will beat us when he gets home."

"Then we shan't be put in the papers?"

"We'll be put to bed!"

The little boy felt pricklings in his nose. He dropped the saw and it fell and splashed their legs with blood.

"Don't you think that hole's big enough for the batteries to come out of?"

He tried to point at the untidy wound in Peter's leg, but he gave it up because his arm was too heavy.

"Perhaps," said his brother, no longer caring. He pulled the handkerchief roughly out of Peter's mouth, but the mouth did not shut. The boy lay staring up at the ceiling and did not even trouble to shut his mouth.

"How silly he looks," the elder brother said contemptuously.

"But he is silly. All that about the horse . . ."

"You can go home now," the elder said to Peter. "Your leg's sawn off enough."

"But we'll have to untie him first . . ."

"Can't he do it himself, the baby?"

He began tugging feverishly at the clothesline, which wrapped itself round them both like a lasso. He used such a bad swearword that his

9

younger brother looked at him in admiration. At last they had finished, but Peter still lay there with empty eyes, his mouth open.

"He doesn't move," said the small boy in a puzzled voice.

"No, you can see he's as dead as a doornail."

"Is he . . . really dead?"

"Of course he's dead. If only he'd kept still. Of course the bactilla couldn't be expected to wait while we tied up such an idiot."

"But . . . can't he come alive again?"

"Of course he can't come alive again when he's dead of blood poisoning. Just take a look at all this."

The younger boy looked and promptly wetted his trousers. It ran down his leg and dripped into the blood and he began to cry so his brother should not hear it dripping.

"Shut up! We must clear this up before mother gets home. Take the kid and throw him out in the road, he's no good to anyone now. I'll have to clean up the floor, because that's something you can't do."

"But I can't carry him on my own . . . it was you who wanted to do this . . . it's your saw . . ."

"Shut up, you crybaby. Drag him away, then. But mind no one sees you . . . or they'll think we killed him . . . and we'll be put in prison."

"But . . . he died of blood poisoning."

10

"Do you think they'll have the sense to see that. Come on!"

He pulled at the body. It fell on the floor and blood spurted on the wall and he screamed with fear.

"You clumsy thing!" his brother shouted.

"Is that all you've done?" he asked when he got back. His brother was on his knees scrubbing hard, but to no avail. The floor was just as red as before.

"What shall I do?" His voice trembled and the younger boy heard with triumph that he was near to crying.

"No one saw me. I threw him into the road. He didn't say anything. Anyway I'm too big to listen to all his silly tales about horses."

They tried to lift the pail and throw the coloured water down the sink. There was a ring at the door.

"We won't open it!"

The little boy wetted his trousers again and looked imploringly at his brother, who did it too. The ringing went on. He went and peeped out from behind the curtains but came back at once.

"It's . . . it's the police."

"What did I tell you," hissed his big brother, and he suddenly noticed that this was quite a new brother, one with a crooked mouth.

"They'll think it's us."

His brother was silent, he was looking at the floor again.

"We must clear this up," he said suddenly, and started scrubbing away at the thick blood like one possessed. The ringing at the door went on.

"They'll come in. They'll break down the door," whimpered the little boy, trembling all over. "They'll take us away. It was you who began it."

"It's only mother," his brother said and suddenly smiled and was himself again except for his red face. But that mother would wash off.

"Mother," he called.

"I've only just got home," mother said outside.

"Well," said the policeman, "a little boy's just been run over outside your house. The car didn't stop and no one saw it happen."

"It couldn't be . . . not one of mine."

Somebody tried the door. The elder boy pulled his brother out of the kitchen and slammed the door shut behind them.

"Thank God," gasped their mother and kissed them both. It was then she got some of the blood on herself.

"But how on earth did you get like this?"

The boys said nothing.

"You're all red . . . has something happened . . . does it hurt?"

The boys did not answer her.

"Tell me, are you alive . . . was it you who were run over?"

"Yes, mother," said the elder boy and began to cry.

"Me too," said his brother and began to cry as well. "Right over."

"Come and let me wash you."

Their mother jerked open the kitchen door and blood welled round her feet and lay caked on the walls.

"But were you run over in here?"

"Yes, mother," wept the elder brother.

"Both at the same time," wept the little boy.

The policeman appeared suddenly in the doorway. He had the fretsaw in his hand.

"What's this?"

"How should I know?" said the mother. "Now, let me get these two washed."

She washed them as white as angels and put them to bed as they had feared. Nevertheless they were in the papers the next day.

MORE SINNED AGAINST

Karl Edward Wagner

Karl Edward Wagner is the author of the tales of Kane, as close as the sword and sorcery genre has ever come to horror fiction. He writes overt horror fiction too, collected as *In a Lonely Place*, and edits *The Year's Best Horror Stories*. The drawback is that he won't include his own stories in his annual anthologies, where they deserve to appear. "More Sinned Against" was commissioned for a recent anthology of unpublished horror fiction, but the editor rejected it on the grounds that it might encourage young readers to take drugs, a curious assumption. It has appeared only in the Scream/Press hardcover of *In a Lonely Place*.

THEIRS WAS A story so commonplace that it balanced uneasily between the maudlin and the sordid—a cliché dipped in filth.

Her real name was Katharina Oglethorpe and she changed that to Candace Thornton when she moved to Los Angeles, but she was known as Candi Thorne in the few films she ever made— the ones that troubled to list credits. She came from some little Baptist church and textile mill town in eastern North Carolina, although later she said she came from Charlotte. She always insisted that her occasional and transient friends call her Candace, and she signed her name Candace in a large, legible hand for those occasional and compulsive autographs. She had lofty aspirations and only minimal talent. One of her former agents perhaps stated her *mot juste*: a lady with a lot of guts, but too much heart. The police records gave her name as Candy Thorneton.

There had been money once in her family, and with that the staunch pride that comes of having more money than the other thousand or so inhabitants of the town put together. Foreign textiles eventually closed the mill; unfortunate investments leeched the money. Pride of place remained.

By the time that any of her past really matters, Candace had graduated from an area church-supported junior college, where she was home-coming queen, and she'd won one or two regional beauty contests and was almost a runner-up in the Miss North Carolina pageant. Her figure was good, although more for a truckstop waitress than suited to a model's re-quirements, and her acting talents were whole-hearted, if marginal. Her parents believed she was safely enrolled at U.C.L.A., and they never quite forgave her when they eventually learned otherwise.

Their tuition checks kept Candace afloat as an aspiring young actress/model through a succes-sion of broken promises, phony deals, and pred-atory agents. Somewhere along the way she sacrificed her cherished virginity a dozen times over, enough so that it no longer pained her, even as the next day dulled the pain of the promised break that never materialized. Her family might have taken back, if not welcomed, their prodigal daughter, had Candace not begged them for money for her first abortion. They refused, Candace got the money anyway, and her family had no more to do with her ever.

He called himself Richards Justin, and there was as much truth to that as to anything else he ever said. He met Candace when she was just on the brink of putting her life together, although he never blamed himself for her subsequent crash. He always said that he was a man who learned from the mistakes of others, and had he said "profited" instead, he might have told the truth for once.

They met because they were sleeping with the same producer, both of them assured of a part in his next film. The producer failed to honor either bargain, and he failed to honor payment for a kilo of coke, after which a South American entrepreneur emptied a Browning Hi-Power into him. Candace and Richards Justin consoled one another over lost opportunity, and afterward he moved in with her.

Candace was sharing a duplex in Venice with two cats and a few thousand roaches. It was a cottage of rotting pink stucco that resembled a gingerbread house left out in the rain. Beside it ran a refuse-choked ditch that had once been a canal. The shack two doors down had been burned out that spring in a shoot-out between rival gangs of bikers. The neighborhood was scheduled for gentrification, but no one had decided yet whether this should entail restoration or razing. The rent was cheaper than an apartment, and against the house grew a massive clump of jade plant that Candace liked to pause before and admire.

At this time Candace was on an upswing and reasonably confident of landing the part of a major victim in a minor stalk-and-slash film. Her face and teeth had always been good; afternoons in the sun and judicious use of rinses on her mousy hair had transformed her into a passable replica of a Malibu blonde. She had that sort of ample figure that looks better with less clothing and best with none at all, and she managed quite well in a few photo spreads in some of the raunchier skin magazines. She was not to be trusted with a speaking part, but some voice and drama coaching might have improved that difficulty in time.

Richards Justin—Rick to his friends—very studiously was a hunk, to use the expression of the moment. He stood six foot four and packed about 215 pounds of health club-nurtured muscle over wide shoulders and lean hips. His belly was quite hard and flat, his thighs strong from jogging, and an even tan set off the generous dark growth of body hair. His black hair was neatly permed, and the heavy mustache added virility to features that stopped just short of being pretty. He seemed designed for posing in tight jeans, muscular arms folded across hairy chest, and he often posed just so. He claimed to have had extensive acting experience in New York before moving to Los Angeles, but somehow his credentials were never subject to verification.

Candace was a type who took in stray animals, and she took in Richards Justin. She had survived two years on the fringes of Hollywood, and Rick was new to Los Angeles—still vulnerable in his search for the elusive Big Break. She was confident that she knew some friends who could help him get started, and she really did need a roommate to help with the rent—once he found work, of course. Rick loaded his suitcase and possessions into her aging Rabbit, with room to spare, and moved in with Candace. He insisted that he pay his share of expenses, and borrowed four hundred bucks to buy some clothes—first appearances count for everything in an interview.

They were great together in bed, and Candace was in love. She recognized the sensitive, lonely soul of the artist hidden beneath his macho exterior. They were both painfully earnest about their acting careers—talking long through the nights of films and actors, great directors and theories of drama. They agreed that one must never compromise art for commercial considerations, but that sometimes it might be necessary to make small compromises in order to achieve the Big Break.

The producer of the stalk-and-slash flick decided that Candace retained too much southern accent for a major role. Having just gone through her savings, Candace spent a vigorous all-night interview with the producer and salvaged a minor role. It wasn't strickly nonspeaking, as she got to scream quite a lot while the deranged killer spiked her to a barn door with a pitchfork. It was quite effective, and a retouched still of her big scene was used for the posters of *Camp Hell!* It was the high-water mark of her career.

Rick found the Big Break even more elusive than a tough, cynical, streetwise hunk like himself had envisioned. It discouraged the artist within him, just as it embarrassed his virile nature to have to live off Candace's earnings continually. Fortunately coke helped restore his confidence, and unfortunately coke was expensive. They both agreed, however, that coke was a necessary expense, careerwise. Coke was both inspiration and encouragement; besides, an actor who didn't have a few grams to flash around was as plausible as an outlaw biker who didn't drink beer.

Candace knew how discouraging this all must be for Rick. In many ways she was so much wiser and tougher than Rick. Her concern over his difficulties distracted her from the disappointment of her own faltering career. Granted, Rick's talents were a bit raw—he was a gem in need of polishing. Courses and workshops were available, but these cost money, too. Candace worked her contacts and changed her agent. If she didn't mind doing a little T&A, her new agent felt sure he could get her a small part or two in some soft-R films. It was money.

Candace played the dumb southern blonde in *Jiggle High* and she played the dumb southern cheerleader in *Cheerleader Superbowl* and she played the dumb southern stewardess in *First Class Only* and she played the dumb southern nurse in *Sex Clinic* and she played the dumb southern hooker in *Hard Streets*, but always this was Candi Thorne who played these roles, and not Candace Thornton, and somehow this made the transition from soft-R to hard-R films a little easier to bear.

They had their first big quarrel when Candace balked over her part in *Malibu Hustlers*. She hadn't realized they were shooting it in both R- and X-rated versions. Prancing about in the buff and faking torrid love scenes was one thing, but Candace drew the line at actually screwing for the close-up cameras. Her agent swore he was through if she backed out of the contract. Rick yelled at her and slapped her around a little, then broke into tears. He hadn't meant to lose control—it was just that he was *so* close to getting his break, and without money all they'd worked so hard together for, all they'd hoped and prayed for . . .

Candace forgave him, and blamed herself for being thoughtless and selfish. If she could ball off camera to land a role, she could give the same performance on camera. This once.

Candace never did find out what her agent did with her check from *Malibu Hustlers*, nor did the police ever manage to find her agent. The producer was sympathetic, but not legally responsible. He did, however, hate to see a sweet kid burned like that, and he offered her a lead role in *Hot 'n' Horny*. This one would be straight X—or XXX, as they liked to call them now—but a lot of talented girls had made the big time doing their stuff for the screen, and Candi Thorne just might be the next super-X superstar. He had the right connections, and if she played it right with him . . .

It wasn't the Big Break Candace had dreamed of, but it was money. And they *did* need money. She worried that this would damage her chances for a legitimate acting career, but Rick told her to stop being a selfish prude and to think of their future together. His break was coming soon, and then they'd never have to worry again about money. Besides, audiences were already watching her perform in *Malibu Hustlers*, so what did she have left to be shy about?

The problem with coke was that Rick needed a lot of it to keep him and his macho image going. The trouble with a lot of coke was that Rick tended to get wired a little too tight, and then he needed downers to mellow out. Smack worked best, but the trouble with smack was that it was even more expensive. Still, tomorrow's male sex symbol couldn't go about dropping ludes and barbs like some junior high punker. Smack was status in this game— everybody did coke. Not to worry: Rick had been doing a little heroin ever since his New York days—no needle work, just some to toot. He could handle it.

Candace could not—either the smack or the expense. Rick was gaining a lot of influential contacts. He had to dress well, show up at the right parties. Sometimes they decided it would be better for his career if he went alone. They really needed a better place to live, now that they could afford it.

After making *Wet 'n' Willing* Candace managed to rent a small house off North Beverly

Glen Boulevard—not much of an improvement over her duplex in Venice, but the address was a quantum leap in class. Her biggest regret was having to leave her cats: no pets allowed. Her producer had advanced her some money to cover immediate expenses, and she knew he'd be getting it back in pounds of flesh. There were parties for important friends, and Candace felt quite casual about performing on camera after some of the things she'd been asked to do on those nights. And that made it easier when she was asked to do them again on camera.

Candace couldn't have endured it all if it weren't for her selfless love for Rick, and for the coke and smack and pills and booze. Rick expressed concern over her increasing use of drugs, especially when they were down to their last few lines. Candace economized by shooting more—less waste and a purer high than snorting.

She was so stoned on the set for *Voodoo Vixens* that she could barely go through the motions of the minimal plot. The director complained; her producer reminded her that retakes cost money, and privately noted that her looks were distinctly taking a shopworn plunge. When she threw up in her costar's lap, he decided that Candi Thorne really wasn't star material.

Rick explained that he was more disappointed than angry with her over getting canned, but this was after he'd bloodied her lip. It wasn't so much that this financial setback stood to wreck his career just as the breaks were falling in place for him, as it was that her drug habit had left them owing a couple thou to the man, and how were they going to pay that?

Candace still had a few contacts to fall back on, and she was back before the cameras before the bruises had disappeared. These weren't the films that made the adult theater circuits. These were the fifteen-minute-or-so single-takes shot in motel rooms for the 8-mm. home projector/porno peep show audiences. Her contacts were pleased to get a seminame porno queen, however semi and however shopworn, even if the films seldom bothered to list credits or titles. It was easier to work with a pro than some drugged-out runaway or amateur hooker, who might ruin a take if the action got rough or she had a phobia about Dobermans.

It was quick work and quick bucks. But not enough bucks.

Rick was panic-stricken when two large black gentlemen stopped him outside a singles bar one night to discuss his credit and to share ideas as to the need to maintain intact kneecaps in this cruel world. They understood a young actor's difficulties in meeting financial obligations, but felt certain Rick could make a substantial payment within forty-eight hours.

Candace hit the streets. It was that, or see Rick maimed. After the casting couch and exotic partners under floodlights, somehow it seemed so commonplace doing quickies in motel rooms and car seats. She missed the cameras. It all seemed so transient without any playback.

The money was there, and Rick kept his kneecaps. Between her work on the streets and grinding out a few 8-mm. films each month, Candace could about meet expenses. The problem was that she really needed the drugs to keep her going, and the more drugs she needed meant the more work to pay for them. Candace knew her looks were slipping, and she appreciated Rick's concern for her health. But for Rick the Big Break was coming soon. She no longer minded when he had other women over while she was on the streets, or when he stayed away for a day or two without calling her. She was selling her body for his career, and she must understand that sometimes it was necessary for Rick, too, to sleep around. In the beginning, some small compromises are to be expected.

A pimp beat her up one night. He didn't like freelance chippies taking johns from his girls on his turf. He would have just scared her, had she agreed to become one of his string, but she needed all her earnings for Rick, and the truth was the pimp considered her just a bit too far-gone to be worth his trouble. So he worked her over but didn't mess up her face too badly, and Candace was able to work again after only about a week.

She tried another neighborhood and got busted the second night out; paid her own bail, got busted again a week later. Rick got her out of jail—she was coming apart without the H, and he couldn't risk being implicated. He had his career to think about, and it was thoughtless of Candace to jeopardize his chances through her own sordid lifestyle.

He would have thrown her out, but Candace paid the rent. Of course, he still loved her. But she really ought to take better care of herself. She was letting herself go. Since her herpes scare they seldom made love, although Candace understood that Rick was often emotionally and physically drained after concentrating his energy on some important interview or audition.

They had lived together almost two years, and Candace was almost 25, but she looked almost 40. After a client broke her nose and a few teeth in a moment of playfulness, she lost what little remained of her actress/model good looks. They got the best cosmetic repair she could afford, but after that neither the johns nor the sleaze producers paid her much attention. When she saw herself on the screen at fifth-rate porno houses, in the glimpses between ducking below the rows of shabby seats, she no longer recognized herself.

But Rick's career was progressing all the while, and that was what made her sacrifice worthwhile. A part of Candace realized now that her dreams of Hollywood stardom had long since washed down the gutter, but at least Rick was almost on the verge of big things. He'd landed a number of modeling jobs and already had made some commercials for local tv. Some recent roles in what Rick termed "experimental theater" promised to draw the attention of talent scouts. Neither of them doubted that the Big Break was an imminent certainty. Candace kept herself going through her faith in Rick's love and her confidence that better times lay ahead. Once Rick's career took off, she'd quit the streets, get off the drugs. She'd look ten years younger if she could just rest and eat right for a few months, get a better repair on her nose. By then Rick would be in a position to help her resume her own acting career.

Candace was not too surprised when Rick came in one morning and shook her awake with the news that he'd lined up a new film for her. It was something about devil worshipers called *Satan's Sluts*—X-rated, of course, but the money would be good, and Candace hadn't appeared even in a peep show gang-bang in a couple months. The producer, Rick explained, remembered her in *Camp Hell!* and was willing to take a chance on giving her a big role.

Candace might have been more concerned about filming a scene with so small a crew and in a cellar made over into a creepy B&D dungeon, but her last films had been shot in cheap motel rooms with a home video camera. She didn't like being strapped to an inverted cross and hung before a black-draped altar, but Rick was there—snorting coke with the half-dozen members of the cast and crew.

When the first few whiplashes cut into her flesh, it took Candace's drugged consciousness several moments to be aware of the pain, and to understand the sort of film for which Rick had sold her. By the time they had heated the branding iron and brought in the black goat, Candace was giving the performance of her life.

She passed out eventually, awoke another day in their bed, vaguely surprised to be alive. It was a measure of Rick's control over Candace that they hadn't killed her. No one was going to pay much attention to anything Candace might say—a burned-out porno star and drug addict with an arrest record for prostitution. Rick had toyed with selling her for a snuff film, but his contacts there preferred anonymous runaways and wetbacks, and the backers of *Satan's Sluts* had paid extra to get a name actress, however

faded, to add a little class to the production—
especially a star who couldn't cause problems
afterward.

Rick stayed with her just long enough to feel
sure she wouldn't die from her torture, and to
pack as many of his possessions as he considered
worth keeping. Rick had been moving up in the
world on Candace's earnings—meeting the
right people, making the right connections. The
money from *Satan's Sluts* had paid off his debts
with enough left over for a quarter-ounce of
some totally awesome rock, which had so im-
pressed his friends at a party that a rising tv
director wanted Rick to move in with her while
they discussed a part for him in a much talked-
about new miniseries.

The pain when he left her was the worst of all.
Rick had counted on this, and he left her with a
gram of barely cut heroin, deciding to let nature
take its course.

Candace had paid for it with her body and her
soul, but at last this genuinely was the Big Break.
The prime-time soaper miniseries, *Destiny's Fortune*, ran for five nights and topped the ratings
each night. Rick's role as the tough steelworker
who romanced the mill owner's daughter in
parts four and five, while not a major part,
attracted considerable attention and benefited
from the huge success of the series itself. Talent

scouts saw a new hunk in Richards Justin, most talked-about young star from the all-time hit, *Destiny's Fortune.*

Rick's new agent knew how to hitch his Mercedes to a rising star. Richards Justin made the cover of *TV Guide* and *People*, the centerfold of *Playgirl*, and then the posters. Within a month it was evident from the response to *Destiny's Fortune* that Richards Justin was a hot property. It was only a matter of casting him for the right series. Network geniuses juggled together all the ingredients of recent hits and projected a winner for the new season—*Colt Savage, Soldier of Fortune.*

They ran the pilot as a two-hour special against a major soaper and a tv-movie about teenage prostitutes, and *Colt Savage* blew the other two networks away in that night's ratings. *Colt Savage* was The New Hit, blasting to the top of the Nielsens on its first regular night. The show borrowed from everything that had already been proven to work—"an homage to the great adventure classics of the '30s" was how its producers liked to describe it.

Colt Savage, as portrayed by Richards Justin, was a tough, cynical, broad-shouldered American adventurer who kept busy dashing about the cities and exotic places of the 1930s—finding lost treasures, battling spies and sinister cults, rescuing plucky young ladies from all manner of dire fates. Colt Savage was the *protege* of a brilliant scientist who wished to devote his vast fortune and secret inventions to fighting Evil. He flew an autogiro and drove a streamlined speedster—both decked out with fantastic weapons and gimmickry rather in advance of the technology of the period. He had a number of exotic assistants and, inevitably, persistent enemies—villains who somehow managed to escape the explosion of their headquarters in time to pop up again two episodes later.

Colt Savage was pure B-movie corn. In a typical episode, Colt would meet a beautiful girl who would ask him for help, then be kidnapped. Following that there would be fights, car chases, air battles, captures and escapes, derring-do in exotic locales, rescues and romance—enough to fill an hour show. The public loved it. Richards Justin was a new hero for today's audiences —the new Bogart, a John Wayne for the '80s. The network promoted *Colt Savage* with every excess at its command. The merchandising rights alone were bringing in tens of millions.

Rick dumped the director who had given him his start in *Destiny's Fortune* long before he moved into several million bucks' worth of Beverly Hills real estate. The tabloids followed his numerous love affairs with compulsive and imaginative interest.

* * *

Candace blamed it all on the drugs. She couldn't bring herself to believe that Rick had never loved her, that he had simply used her until she had no more to give. Her mind refused to accept that. It was she who had let Rick down, let drugs poison his life and destroy hers. Drugs had ruined her acting career, had driven her onto the streets to pay for their habit. They could have made it, if she hadn't ruined everything for them.

So she quit, cold turkey. Broken in body and spirit, the miseries of withdrawal made little difference to her pain. She lived ten years of hell over the next few days, lying in an agonized delirium that barely distinguished consciousness from unconsciousness. Sometimes she managed to crawl to the bathroom or to the refrigerator, mostly she just curled herself into a fetal pose of pain and shivered beneath the sweaty sheets and bleeding sores. In her nightmares she drifted from lying in Rick's embrace to writhing in torture on Satan's altar, and the torment of either delirium was the same to her.

As soon as she was strong enough to face it, Candace cut the heroin Rick had left her to make five grams and sold it to one of her friends who liked to snort it and wouldn't mind the cut. It gave her enough money to cover bills until Candace was well enough to be back on the streets. She located the pimp who had once beat her up; he didn't recognize her, and when Candace asked to work for him, he laughed her out of the bar.

After that she drifted around Los Angeles for a month or two, turning tricks whenever she could. She was no longer competitive, even without the scars, but she managed to scrape by, somehow making rent for the place on North Beverly Glen. It held her memories of Rick, and if she let that go, she would have lost even that shell of their love. She even refused to throw out any of his discarded clothing and possessions; his toothbrush and an old razor still lay by the sink.

The last time the cops busted her, Candace had herpes, a penicillin-resistant clap, and no way of posting bail. Jail meant losing her house and its memories of Rick, and there would be nothing left for her after that. Rick could help her now, but she couldn't manage to reach him. An old mutual friend finally did, but when he came to visit Candace he couldn't bear to give her Rick's message, and so he paid her bail himself and told her the money came from Rick, who didn't want to risk getting his name involved.

She had to have a legitimate job. The friend had a friend who owned an interest in a plastic novelties plant, and they got Candace a factory job there. By now she had very little left of herself to sell in the streets, but at least she was off the drugs. Somewhat to the surprise of all concerned, Candace settled down on the line and turned out to be a good worker. Her job paid the bills, and at night she went home and read about Richards Justin in the papers and magazines, played back video cassettes of him nights when he wasn't on live.

The cruelest thing was that Candace still nurtured the hope that she could win Rick back, once she got her own act together. Regular meals, decent hours, medication and time healed some wounds. That face that looked back at her from mirrors no longer resembled a starved plague victim. Some of the men at the plant were beginning to stare after her, and a couple of times she'd been asked to go out. She might have got over Richards Justin in time, but probably not.

The friend of a friend pulled some strings and called in some favors, and so the plant where Candace worked secured the merchandising rights to the Colt Savage, Soldier of Fortune Action Pak. This consisted of a plastic Colt Savage doll, complete with weapons and action costumes, along with models of Black Blaze, his supersonic autogiro, and Red Lightning, the supercar. The merchandising package also included dolls of his mentor and regular assistants, as well as several notable villains and their sinister weaponry. The plant geared into maximum production to handle the anticipated rush of orders for the Christmas market.

Candace found herself sitting at the assembly line, watching thousands of plastic replicas of Richards Justin roll past her.

She just had to see Rick, but the guards at the gate had instructions not to admit her. He wouldn't even talk to her over the phone or answer her letters. The way he must remember her, Candace couldn't really blame him. It would be different now.

His birthday was coming up, and she knew he would be having a party. She wrote him several times, sent messages via old contacts, begging Rick to let her come. When the printed invitation finally came, she'd already bought him a present. Candace knew that her confidence had not been a mistake, and she took a day off work to get ready for their evening together.

The party had been going strong for some time when Candace arrived, and Rick was flying high on coke and champagne. He hugged her around the shoulders but didn't kiss her, and half carried her over to where many of the guests were crowded around a projection television.

Ladies and gentlemen, here she is—our leading lady, the versatile Miss Candi Thorne.

All eyes flicked from the screen to Candace, long enough for recognition. Then the cheers and applause burst out across the room. Rick had been amusing his guests with some of her films. Just now they were watching the one with the donkey.

Candace didn't really remember how she managed to escape and find her way home.

She decided not to leave a note, and she was prying the blade out of Rick's old razor when the idea began to form. The razor was crudded with dried lather and bits of Rick's whiskers, and she wanted to get it clean before she used it on her wrists. A scene from another of her films, *Voodoo Vixens*, arose through the confusion of her thoughts. She set the razor aside carefully.

Candace made herself a cup of coffee and let the idea build in her head. She was dry-eyed now and quite calm—the hysterical energy that had driven her to suicide now directed her disordered thoughts toward another course of action.

She still had all of her mementos of Rick, and throughout the night she went over them, one by one, coolly and meticulously. She scraped all the bits of beard and skin from his razor, collected hair and dandruff from his brush and comb, pared away his toothbrush bristles for the minute residues of blood and plaque. She found a discarded handkerchief, stained from a coke-induced nosebleed, and from the mattress liner came residues of their former lovemaking. Old clothes yielded bits of hair, stains of body oils and perspiration. Candace searched the house relentlessly, finding fragments of his nails, his hair, anything at all that retained physical residues of Rick's person.

The next day Candace called in sick. She spent the day browsing through Los Angeles' numerous occult bookshops, made a few purchases, and called up one or two of the contacts she'd made filming *Voodoo Vixens*. It all seemed straightforward enough. Even those who rationalized it all admitted that it was a matter of belief. And children have the purest belief in magic.

Candace ground up all her bits and scrapings of Richards Justin. It came to quite a pile and reminded her of a bag of Mexican heroin.

Candace returned to work and waited for her chance. When no one was watching, she dumped her powdered residue into the plastic muck destined to become Colt Savage dolls. Then she said a prayer of sorts.

Beneath the Christmas tree, Joshua plays with his new Colt Savage doll. *Pow!* An electron cannon knocks Colt out of the sky, crashes him to the rocks below!

Jason pits Colt Savage against his model dinosaurs. *Yahhh!* The dinosaur stomps him!

David is racing Colt Savage in his car, Red

Lightning. *Ker-blam!* Colt drives off the cliff at a hundred miles an hour!

Billy is still too young to play with his Colt Savage doll, but he likes to chew on it.

Mark decides to see if Colt Savage and Black Blaze can withstand the attack of his atomic bomb firecrackers.

Jessica is mad at her brother. She sees his Colt Savage doll and stomps on it as hard as she can.

Tyrone is bawling. He pulled the arms off his Colt Savage doll, and he can't make them go back on.

Richards Justin collapsed on set, and only heavy sedation finally stilled his screams. It quickly became apparent that his seizures were permanent, and he remains under sedation in a psychiatric institution. Doctors have attributed his psychotic break to long-term drug abuse.

Nothing excites the public more than a fallen hero. *Richards Justin: The Untold Story*, by Candace Thornton, rose quickly on the best-seller charts. Reportedly she was recently paid well over a million for the film rights to her book.

LOST MEMORY
Peter Phillips

Peter Phillips is a British newspaperman who published several noted science fiction stories in the late forties and early fifties. "Dreams are Sacred" is probably the best known, but "Lost Memory" is at least as powerful. One of the genres horror fiction sometimes encompasses is science fiction, and the following tale is certainly one example. Peter Phillips tells me that he may be writing some new horror stories soon, and I very much hope he does.

I COLLAPSED JOINTS and hung up to talk with Dak-whirr. He blinked his eyes in some discomfort.

"What do you want, Palil?" he asked complainingly.

"As if you didn't know."

"I can't give you permission to examine it. The thing is being saved for inspection by the board. What guarantee do I have that you won't spoil it for them?"

I thrust confidentially at one of his body-plates. "You owe me a favor," I said. "Remember?"

"That was a long time in the past."

45

"Only two thousand revolutions and a reassembly ago. If it wasn't for me, you'd be eroding in a pit. All I want is a quick look at its thinking part. I'll vrull the consciousness without laying a single pair of pliers on it."

He went into a feedback twitch, an indication of the conflict between his debt to me and his self-conceived duty.

Finally he said, "Very well, but keep tuned to me. If I warn that a board member is coming, remove yourself quickly. Anyway, how do you know it has consciousness? It may be mere primal metal."

"In that form? Don't be foolish. It's obviously a manufacture. And I'm not conceited enough to believe that we are the only form of intelligent manufacture in the Universe."

"Tautologous phrasing, Palil," Dak-whirr said pedantically. "There could not conceivably be 'unintelligent manufacture.' There can be no consciousness without manufacture, and no manufacture without intelligence. Therefore there can be no consciousness without intelligence. Now if you should wish to dispute—"

I turned off his frequency abruptly and hurried away. Dak-whirr is a fool and a bore. Everyone knows there's a fault in his logic circuit, but he refuses to have it traced down and repaired. Very unintelligent of him.

* * *

The thing had been taken into one of the museum sheds by the carriers. I gazed at it in admiration for some moments. It was quite beautiful, having suffered only slight exterior damage, and it was obviously no mere conglomeration of sky metal.

In fact, I immediately thought of it as "he" and endowed it with the attributes of self-knowing, although, of course, his consciousness could not be functioning or he would have attempted communication with us.

I fervently hoped that the board, after his careful disassembly and study, could restore his awareness so that he could tell us himself which solar system he came from.

Imagine it! He had achieved our dream of many thousands of revolutions—spaceflight—only to be fused, or worse, in his moment of triumph.

I felt a surge of sympathy for the lonely traveler as he lay there, still, silent, nonemitting. Anyway, I mused, even if we couldn't restore him to self-knowing, an analysis of his construction might give us the secret of the power he had used to achieve the velocity to escape his planet's gravity.

In shape and size he was not unlike Swen—or Swen Two, as he called himself after his conversion—who failed so disastrously to reach our satellite, using chemical fuels. But where

Swen Two had placed his tubes, the stranger had a curious helical construction studded at irregular intervals with small crystals.

He was thirty-five feet tall, a gracefully tapering cylinder. Standing at his head, I could find no sign of exterior vision cells, so I assumed he had some kind of vrulling sense. There seemed to be no exterior markings at all, except the long, shallow grooves dented in his skin by scraping to a stop along the hard surface of our planet.

I am a reporter with warm current in my wires, not a cold-thinking scientist, so I hesitated before using my own vrulling sense. Even though the stranger was nonaware—perhaps permanently—I felt it would be a presumption, an invasion of privacy. There was nothing else I could do, though, of course.

I started to vrull, gently at first, then harder, until I was positively glowing with effort. It was incredible; his skin seemed absolutely impermeable.

The sudden realization that metal could be so alien nearly fused something inside me. I found myself backing away in horror, my self-preservation relay working overtime.

Imagine watching one of the beautiful cone-rod-and-cylinder assemblies performing the Dance of the Seven Spanners, as he's conditioned to do, and then suddenly refusing to do anything except stump around unattractively, or even becoming obstinately motionless, unresponsive. That might give you an idea of how I felt in that dreadful moment.

Then I remembered Dak-whirr's words— there could be no such thing as an "unintelligent manufacture." And a product so beautiful could surely not be evil. I overcame my repugnance and approached again.

I halted as an open transmission came from someone near at hand.

"Who gave that squeaking reporter permission to snoop around here?"

I had forgotten the museum board. Five of them were standing in the doorway of the shed, radiating anger. I recognized Chirik, the chairman, and addressed myself to him. I explained that I'd interfered with nothing and pleaded for permission on behalf of my subscribers to watch their investigation of the stranger. After some argument, they allowed me to stay.

I watched in silence and some amusement as one by one they tried to vrull the silent being from space. Each showed the same reaction as myself when they failed to penetrate the skin.

Chirik, who is wheeled—and inordinately vain about his suspension system—flung himself back on his supports and pretended to be thinking.

"Fetch Fiff-fiff," he said at last. "The creature

may still be aware, but unable to communicate on our standard frequencies."

Fiff-fiff can detect anything in any spectrum. Fortunately he was at work in the museum that day and soon arrived in answer to the call. He stood silently near the stranger for some moments, testing and adjusting himself, then slid up the electromagnetic band.

"He's emitting," he said.

"Why can't we get him?" asked Chirik.

"It's a curious signal on an unusual band."

"Well, what does he say?"

"Sounds like utter nonsense to me. Wait, I'll relay and convert it to standard."

I made a direct recording, naturally, like any good reporter.

"—after planetfall," the stranger was saying. "Last dribble of power. If you don't pick this up, my name is Entropy. Other instruments knocked to hell, air lock jammed and I'm too weak to open it manually. Becoming delirious, too, I guess. Getting strong undirectional ultrawave reception in Inglish, craziest stuff you ever heard, like goblins muttering, and I know we were the only ship in this sector. If you pick this up, but can't get a fix in time, give my love to the boys in the mess. Signing off for another couple of hours, but keeping this channel open and hoping . . ."

"The fall must have deranged him," said Chirik, gazing at the stranger. "Can't he see us or hear us?"

"He couldn't hear you properly before, but he can now, through me," Fiff-fiff pointed out. "Say something to him, Chirik."

"Hello," said Chirik doubtfully. "Er— welcome to our planet. We are sorry you were hurt by your fall. We offer you the hospitality of our assembly shops. You will feel better when you are repaired and repowered. If you will indicate how we can assist you—"

"What the hell! What ship is that? Where are you?"

"We're here," said Chirik. "Can't you see us or vrull us? Your vision circuit is impaired, perhaps? Or do you depend entirely on vrulling? We can't find your eyes and assumed either that you protected them in some way during flight, or dispensed with vision cells altogether in your conversion."

Chirik hesitated, continued apologetically: "But we cannot understand how you vrull, either. While we thought that you were unaware, or even completely fused, we tried to vrull you. Your skin is quite impervious to us, however."

The stranger said: "I don't know if you're batty or I am. What distance are you from me?"

Chirik measured quickly. "One meter, two-point-five centimeters from my eyes to your nearest point. Within touching distance, in fact." Chirik tentatively put out his hand. "Can you not feel me, or has your contact sense also been affected?"

It became obvious that the stranger had been pitifully deranged. I reproduce his words phonetically from my record, although some of them make little sense. Emphasis, punctuative pauses and spelling of unknown terms are mere guesswork, of course.

He said: "For godsakemann stop talking nonsense, whoever you are. If you're outside, can't you see the air lock is jammed? Can't shift it myself. I'm badly hurt. Get me out of here, please."

"Get you out of where?" Chirik looked around, puzzled. "We brought you into an open shed near our museum for a preliminary examination. Now that we know you're intelligent, we shall immediately take you to our assembly shops for healing and recuperation. Rest assured that you'll have the best possible attention."

There was a lengthy pause before the stranger spoke again, and his words were slow and deliberate. His bewilderment is understandable, I believe, if we remember that he could not see, vrull or feel.

He asked: "What manner of creature are you? Describe yourself."

Chirik turned to us and made a significant gesture toward his thinking part, indicating gently that the injured stranger had to be humored.

"Certainly," he replied. "I am an unspecialized bipedal manufacture of standard proportions, lately self-converted to wheeled traction, with a hydraulic suspension system of my own devising which I'm sure will interest you when we restore your sense circuits."

There was an even longer silence.

"You are robots," the stranger said at last. "Crise knows how you got here or why you speak Inglish, but you must try to understand me. I am mann. I am a friend of your master, your maker. You must fetch him to me at once."

"You are not well," said Chirik firmly. "Your speech is incoherent and without meaning. Your fall has obviously caused several feedbacks of a very serious nature. Please lower your voltage. We are taking you to our shops immediately. Reserve your strength to assist our specialists as best you can in diagnosing your troubles."

"Wait. You must understand. You are— ogodno that's no good. Have you no memory of mann? The words you use—what meaning have they for you? *Manufacture*—made by hand hand hand damyou. *Healing*. Metal is not healed. *Skin*.

53

Skin is not metal. *Eyes.* Eyes are not scanning cells. Eyes grow. Eyes are soft. My eyes are soft. Mine eyes have seen the glory—steady on, sun. Get a grip. Take it easy. You out there listen."

"Out where?" asked Prrr-chuk, deputy chairman of the museum board.

I shook my head sorrowfully. This was nonsense, but, like any good reporter, I kept my recorder running.

The mad words flowed on. "You call me he. Why? You have no seks. You are knewter. You are *it it it!* I am he, he who made you, sprung from shee, born of wumman. What is wumman, who is silvya what is shee that all her swains commend her ogod the bluds flowing again. Remember. Think back, you out there. These words were made by mann, for mann. Hurt, healing, hospitality, horror, deth by loss of blud. *Deth. Blud.* Do you understand these words? Do you remember the soft things that made you? Soft little mann who konkurred the Galaxy and made sentient slaves of his machines and saw the wonders of a million worlds, only this miserable representative has to die in lonely desperation on a far planet, hearing goblin voices in the darkness."

Here my recorder reproduces a most curious sound, as though the stranger were using an ancient type of vibratory molecular vocalizer in a gaseous medium to reproduce his words before transmission, and the insulation on his diaphragm had come adrift.

It was a jerky, high-pitched, strangely disturbing sound; but in a moment the fault was corrected and the stranger resumed transmission.

"Does blud mean anything to you?"

"No," Chirik replied simply.

"Or deth?"

"No."

"Or wor?"

"Quite meaningless."

"What is your origin? How did you come into being?"

"There are several theories," Chirik said. "The most popular one—which is no more than a grossly unscientific legend, in my opinion—is that our manufacturer fell from the skies, imbedded in a mass of primal metal on which He drew to erect the first assembly shop. How He came into being is left to conjecture. My own theory, however—"

"Does legend mention the shape of this primal metal?"

"In vague terms, yes. It was cylindrical, of vast dimensions."

"An interstellar vessel," said the stranger.

"That is my view also," said Chirik complacently. "And—"

"What was the supposed appearance of your —manufacturer?"

"He is said to have been of magnificent proportions, based harmoniously on a cubical plan, static in Himself, but equipped with a vast array of senses."

"An automatic computer," said the stranger.

He made more curious noises, less jerky and at a lower pitch than the previous sounds.

He corrected the fault and went on: "God that's funny. A ship falls, menn are no more, and an automatic computer has pupps. Oh, yes, it fits in. A self-setting computer and navigator, operating on verbal orders. It learns to listen for itself and know itself for what it is, and to absorb knowledge. It comes to hate menn—or at least their bad qualities—so it deliberately crashes the ship and pulps their puny bodies with a calculated nicety of shock. Then it propagates and does a dam fine job of selective erasure on whatever it gave its pupps to use for a memory. It passes on only the good it found in mann, and purges the memory of him completely. Even purges all of his vocabulary except scientific terminology. Oil is thicker than blud. So may they live without the burden of knowing that they are—ogod they must know, they must understand. You outside, what happened to this manufacturer?"

Chirik, despite his professed disbelief in the

supernormal aspects of the ancient story, automatically made a visual sign of sorrow.

"Legend has it," he said, "that after completing His task, He fused himself beyond possibility of healing."

Abrupt, low-pitched noises came again from the stranger. "Yes. He would. Just in case any of His pupps should give themselves forbidden knowledge and an infeeryorrity komplecks by probing his mnemonic circuits. The perfect self-sacrificing muther. What sort of environment did He give you? Describe your planet."

Chirik looked around at us again in bewilderment, but he replied courteously, giving the stranger a description of our world.

"Of course," said the stranger. "Of course. Sterile rock and metal suitable only for you. But there must be some way . . ."

He was silent for a while.

"Do you know what growth means?" he asked finally. "Do you have anything that grows?"

"Certainly," Chirik said helpfully. "If we should suspend a crystal of some substance in a saturated solution of the same element or compound—"

"No, no," the stranger interrupted. "Have you nothing that grows of itself, that fruktiffies and gives increase without your intervention?"

"How could such a thing be?"

"Criseallmytee I should have guessed. If you had one blade of gras, just one tiny blade of growing gras, you could extrapolate from that to me. Green things, things that feed on the rich brest of erth, cells that divide and multiply, a cool grove of treez in a hot summer, with tiny warmbludded burds preening their fethers among the leeves; a feeld of spring weet with newbawn mise timidly threading the dangerous jungul of storks; a stream of living water where silver fish dart and pry and feed and procreate; a farmyard where things grunt and cluck and greet the new day with the stirring pulse of life, with a surge of blud. Blud—"

For some inexplicable reason, although the strength of his carrier wave remained almost constant, the stranger's transmission seemed to be growing fainter.

"His circuits are failing," Chirik said. "Call the carriers. We must take him to an assembly shop immediately. I wish he would reserve his power."

My presence with the museum board was accepted without question now. I hurried along with them as the stranger was carried to the nearest shop.

I now noticed a circular marking in that part of his skin on which he had been resting, and guessed that it was some kind of orifice through which he would have extended his planetary traction mechanism if he had not been injured.

He was gently placed on a disassembly cradle. The doctor in charge that day was Chur-chur, an old friend of mine. He had been listening to the two-way transmissions and was already acquainted with the case.

Chur-chur walked thoughtfully around the stranger.

"We shall have to cut," he said. "It won't pain him, since his intramolecular pressure and contact senses have failed. But since we can't vrull him, it'll be necessary for him to tell us where his main brain is housed or we might damage it."

Fiff-fiff was still relaying, but no amount of power boost would make the stranger's voice any clearer. It was quite faint now, and there are places on my recorder tape from which I cannot make even the roughest phonetic transliteration.

". . . strength going. Can't get into my zoot . . . done for if they bust through lock, done for if they don't . . . must tell them I need oxygen . . ."

"He's in bad shape, desirous of extinction," I remarked to Chur-chur, who was adjusting his arc-cutter. "He wants to poison himself with oxidation now."

I shuddered at the thought of that vile, corrosive gas he had mentioned, which causes that almost unmentionable condition we all fear—rust.

Chirik spoke firmly through Fiff-fiff. "Where is your thinking part, stranger? Your central brain?"

"In my head," the stranger replied. "In my head ogod my head . . . eyes blurring everything going dim . . . luv to mairee . . . kids . . . a carry me home to the lone prayree . . . get this bluddy air lock open then they'll see me die . . . but they'll see me . . . some kind of atmosphere with this gravity . . . see me die . . . extrapolate from body what I was . . . what they are damthem damthem damthem . . . mann . . . master . . . I AM YOUR MAKER!"

For a few seconds the voice rose strong and clear, then faded away again and dwindled into a combination of those two curious noises I mentioned earlier. For some reason that I cannot explain, I found the combined sound very disturbing despite its faintness. It may be that it induced some kind of sympathetic oscillation.

Then came words, largely incoherent and punctuated by a kind of surge like the sonic vibrations produced by variations of pressure in a leaking gas-filled vessel.

". . . done it . . . crawling into chamber, closing inner . . . must be mad . . . they'd find me anyway . . . but finished . . . want see them before I die . . . want see them see me . . . liv few seconds, watch them . . . get outer one open . . ."

Chur-chur had adjusted his arc to a broad, clean, blue-white glare. I trembled a little as he brought it near the edge of the circular marking in the stranger's skin. I could almost feel the disruption of the intramolecular sense currents in my own skin.

"Don't be squeamish, Palil," Chur-chur said kindly. "He can't feel it now that his contact sense has gone. And you heard him say that his central brain is in his head." He brought the cutter firmly up to the skin. "I should have guessed that. He's the same shape as Swen Two, and Swen very logically concentrated his main thinking part as far away from his explosion chambers as possible."

Rivulets of metal ran down into a tray which a calm assistant had placed on the ground for that purpose. I averted my eyes quickly. I could never steel myself enough to be a surgical engineer or assembly technician.

But I had to look again, fascinated. The whole area circumscribed by the marking was beginning to glow.

Abruptly the stranger's voice returned, quite strongly, each word clipped, emphasized, high-pitched.

"Ar no no no . . . god my hands . . . they're burning through the lock and I can't get back I can't get away . . . stop it you feens stop it can't you hear . . . I'll be burned to deth I'm here in the air lock . . . the air's getting hot you're burning me alive . . ."

Although the words made little sense, I could guess what had happened and I was horrified.

"Stop, Chur-chur," I pleaded. "The heat has somehow brought back his skin currents. It's hurting him."

Chur-chur said reassuringly: "Sorry, Palil. It occasionally happens during an operation—probably a local thermoelectric effect. But even if his contact senses have started working again and he can't switch them off, he won't have to bear this very long."

Chirik shared my unease, however. He put out his hand and awkwardly patted the stranger's skin.

"Easy there," he said. "Cut out your senses if you can. If you can't, well, the operation is nearly finished. Then we'll repower you, and you'll soon be fit and happy again, healed and fitted and reassembled."

I decided that I liked Chirik very much just then. He exhibited almost as much self-induced empathy as any reporter; he might even come to like my favorite blue stars, despite his cold scientific exactitude in most respects.

My recorder tape shows, in its reproduction of certain sounds, how I was torn away from this strained reverie.

During the one-and-a-half seconds since I had recorded the distinct vocables "burning me alive," the stranger's words had become quite blurred, running together and rising even higher in pitch until they reached a sustained note—around E-flat in the standard sonic scale.

It was not like a voice at all.

This high, whining noise was suddenly modulated by apparent words, but without changing its pitch. Transcribing what seem to be words is almost impossible, as you can see for yourself—this is the closest I can come phonetically:

"Eeee ahahmbeeeeing baked aliiive in an uvennn ahdeeerjeeesussunmuuutherrr!"

The note swooped higher and higher until it must have neared supersonic range, almost beyond either my direct or recorded hearing.

Then it stopped as quickly as a contact break.

And although the soft hiss of the stranger's carrier wave carried on without perceptible diminution, indicating that some degree of awareness still existed, I experienced at that moment one of those quirks of intuition given only to reporters:

I felt that I would never greet the beautiful stranger from the sky in his full senses.

Chur-chur was muttering to himself about the extreme toughness and thickness of the stranger's skin. He had to make four complete cutting revolutions before the circular mass of nearly white-hot metal could be pulled away by a magnetic grapple.

A billow of smoke puffed out of the orifice. Despite my repugnance, I thought of my duty as a reporter and forced myself to look over Chur-chur's shoulder.

The fumes came from a soft, charred, curiously shaped mass of something which lay just inside the opening.

"Undoubtedly a kind of insulating material," Chur-chur explained.

He drew out the crumpled blackish heap and placed it carefully on a tray. A small portion broke away, showing a red, viscid substance.

"It looks complex," Chur-chur said, "but I expect the stranger will be able to tell us how to reconstitute it or make a substitute."

His assistant gently cleaned the wound of the remainder of the material, which he placed with the rest; and Chur-chur resumed his inspection of the orifice.

You can, if you want, read the technical accounts of Chur-chur's discovery of the stranger's double skin at the point where the cut was made; of the incredible complexity of his driving mechanism, involving principles which are still not understood to this day; of the museum's failure to analyze the exact nature and function of the insulating material found in only that one portion of his body; and of the other scientific mysteries connected with him.

But this is my personal, nonscientific account. I shall never forget hearing about the greatest mystery of all, for which not even the most tentative explanation has been advanced, nor the utter bewilderment with which Chur-chur announced his initial findings that day.

He had hurriedly converted himself to a convenient size to permit actual entry into the stranger's body.

When he emerged, he stood in silence for several minutes. Then, very slowly, he said:

"I have examined the 'central brain' in the forepart of his body. It is no more than a simple auxiliary computer mechanism. It does not possess the slightest trace of consciousness. And there is no other conceivable center of intelligence in the remainder of his body."

There is something I wish I could forget. I can't explain why it should upset me so much. But I always stop the tape before it reaches the point where the voice of the stranger rises in pitch, going higher and higher until it cuts out.

There's a quality about that noise that makes me tremble and think of rust.

THE FIFTH MASK

Shamus Frazer

Robert Aickman was wont to point out how many writers, prolific and popular in their time, are remembered only for their ghost stories. He took this to demonstrate the lasting worth of the genre at its best, and I agree with him. Shamus Frazer wrote novels once upon a time, but I venture to suggest that he will be remembered longest for "The Fifth Mask." I encountered it twenty-five years or more ago, in the *London Mystery Magazine*, and it has stayed with me ever since.

REMEMBER, REMEMBER—THE Fifth of November? I only wish it were possible to forget it. But every year at this time one is reminded of what has been, and—*of what is to come*. The squibs crackle in the fog-shrouded alleys even before October is out; there is the tang of gunpowder in the sharpening air; the frontier incidents of memory, these—the skirmishing before the campaign opens in evil earnest.

I keep to the highways at this season. But even in the Strand, among the neon lights, one runs into those little grim cortèges out of their rat holes in the river fog: the cork-blackened faces, the trundling soapbox trolley, with its stiff, bloated guy bulging the tattered suit, the desperado hat pulled down over the eyeless, unwholesome mask; and no matter how quickly one tries to get by, one doesn't escape that rat squealing chorus, "Spare a penny for the old guy, mister . . ." Like a finger of ice drawn down between the shoulder blades—that's how it takes me.

I hurry past, till the ribaldries flung at my back fall off, and I can pull in my stride and plan how to stop myself thinking.

Oh, I've tried the cinemas—but they're too dark and there's muttering and breathing at your back; and even when the lights are turned on, the faces of the strangers banked around you are like—like masks . . . waiting for the dark, if you see what I mean. So it's usually a pub. Luckily I found this one! I was whacked. All the way along that chant: "Remember, remember . . . *spare a penny for the old guy.*" Then at the corner here . . . just beyond the frosted window there with the goat and the pair of stilts on it—there was a kid standing in a mask; he didn't say anything . . . but when I came by he made as if to take it off—his mask I mean. So I turned in here . . . to be out of the way.

Tumbled in, you say? Well, I tripped over the mat certainly, if that's what you mean. Daft sort of place to put a mat.

Nerves? Well, there's something in that, too— but there's nothing without a reason. That's what's so frightening—just why it should have happened to me; and if there's a reason *there*, mind you, I don't want to know it.

Why should I have been picked on—a mere child? Robin Truby and I couldn't have been more than ten if we were that much when . . . this incident I'd hoped to get out of my mind long since . . . took place.

No, let me stand this one. Two double whiskies, miss. The gentleman's paid, eh? It's kind, very kind—but no cause; the fall shook me up a bit, but I'm all right now. The whisky helps and someone with patience to understand.

Robin? Robin's dead now. At Normandy it was: one of those phosphorus bombs he was carrying, touched off by a bullet—burning with the phosphorus in his guts. You couldn't put it out: like one of those guys they stuff with fireworks, they couldn't get near him. There's only me left: for the time being, that is . . .

We were friends as kids, our parents living next door, see. At Failing this was, in Darkshire. I'm from the North, though you perhaps wouldn't guess it: what with the war and living down here since, I've *changed*. A citizen of no abiding city, that's me—and all of us, if it comes to that. But there's something *real* about the place you've lived in as a child.

You've never visited Failing, I take it? Well, there's not much to see: it's not as if it were London or anything. Industrial, you know:

smoke-blackened chapels, and row upon row of yellow brick houses under blue slate roofs. My folk and Robin Truby's lived cheek by jowl, as the saying has it, in one of these rows—and we were always in and out of each other's houses, or scrambling over the wall that shut off the backyards. Robin was a one for mischief: red hair he had, and a way with it. Robin Hood we called him, and I was Friar Tuck, because I was a well-built lad and on account of my glasses.

Yes, I know: you'll be asking yourself what this has got to do with what I've to talk about—guy, Fifth of November and all? I'm coming to it in my own time, sir—if time is ever our own, that is, and not lent to us, all cut to different lengths as it were. I worked in a draper's once, and . . . but that's not what I've got to make up my mind to tell.

We used to save for the Fifth—Robin and I: save up the pennies and lay in a store of Burmese lights, and bangers, star rockets, Roman candles, Catherine wheels and such, but mostly it was bangers. And for weeks we'd be pestering our dads for an old hat, a pair of trousers with the patch on the seat worn through, a coat with the elbows out—anything that would do for the old guy. We'd get togged up, too, the last few nights . . . in masks . . . and go cadging coppers if we hadn't enough by then: but in a distant part of the town, where we wouldn't be run into by folks we knew. If it had got home what we were doing, we'd have been given a hiding we'd have remembered all our lives. It was *respectable* the district Robin and I lived in, and the worst crime we could commit was behaving like common boys might be expected to behave. That's why we put on those masks . . . so we shouldn't be recognised if a neighbour was to pass.

We bought them at a little newsagent's called Horrobin, where sometimes we'd get a penn'orth of aniseed balls or liquorice sweets when out for a walk this way, to or from the Town Fields. Robin chose a death's-head, greeny white; and mine was a nigger's the time I'm speaking of, liquorice black with red eyeballs; a nigger demon's you might describe it. We put them on outside, and mark this—I had to take my specs off to fit it to the face, and then put them on again over the mask and all so I could see my way, being shortsighted. Robin did look a sight, grisly, with his red hair sitting up like flames atop that green hollow skull-face.

"Here, stick your hat on," I said; and we pulled on the old felt hats with the feather in the band that we'd brought with us. They held the masks more firm to our heads: soft cardboard or a kind of paper-mash they were, with a funny smell to them, sickly.

We had settled to cross the Town Fields to a part where there was a new housing estate—

working-class with shops, a cinema and everything—raised on the old wartime 1914–18 aerodrome. There was no one to know us that side, and we reckoned it would be dark before we came to it.

The Town Fields in Failing have been turned into recreation space now—tennis courts, cricket pavilion, that kind of thing; but at the time I'm speaking of they were under the plough. Often Robin and me would play stalking Indians in the corn there—till one day the farmer caught us at it. But by November of course the corn was gone; I can't recollect what was growing there unless some yellowing stalks and stumps of mangel-wurzel.

It was foggy—not thick but moving in swirls. We kept to the top of the fields. There's a wide path there, with seats set out and gas lamps; set on a ridge, with big villas behind stone walls and tarred-wood fencing one side of it, and their gardens gloomy with tall trees and shrubberies, and the fields dipping below it the other side in a slow wide curve like they were the sea; a real treasure trail for conkers that path in the early autumn—though after . . . after what happened I never cared to visit it again.

It was late afternoon but not dark when Robin and I took our way along this path. We passed the lamplighter with his long pole; but he was early that afternoon, and in the pale dusk the chain of lighted gas lamps he'd left behind him gave more of noise than light, a hissing and plopping as if they were trying to tell you something.

We'd almost got to the stile that led to a footpath cutting down half a mile or more to the bottom of the fields—we weren't in a hurry, mind you—we'd been along there in the dark before, and we'd got our battery flashlights in our pockets; but, speaking for myself, when that voice called to us my first impulse was to scramble over the stile and run and run until I dropped. It was a thin voice and high, and somehow cold, very cold. I'd got my leg over the stile, but in my fright I slipped and fell off. Robin pulled me to my feet again.

"Who was it?" I gasped. "Who was it spoke just now?"

"Don't be a mutt, Fred Tucker. It's only a lady. She doesn't know us," he whispered. "She may be good for a tanner if we try it on—winsome like."

"A Death, a little Death—and are there two?" the thin voice continued. "Is Death that small boy's mate? . . . No, I *see*—a little negro, a Nubian, Death's Ethiopian slave . . ."

She was sitting in the middle of one of those seats I've spoken of; fussy iron painted a dark crimson, that must have been put there the same time as the gas lamps were set up when the

Widow Queen sat at Windsor in crinolines. She was thin as her voice, dressed all in black, a kind of black straw bonnet with a purple velvet ribbon nodding on her head; there was a stucco wall behind her, patched and discoloured as a gravestone, and the ghosts of winter trees rising above and losing themselves in the twilight. I got as big a fright to see her as when I'd first heard her voice—and I'd have bolted but for Robin's grip on my arm. "Come on!" he said, and pinching me as if he'd have me join in with him, called out in a kind of wheedling singsong: "Spare a penny, lady, for the old guy?"

"Which old guy?" she said with a chuckle that set your teeth on edge. "I only see two young ones, but my eyes are not as good as they were . . . *in the dark!*" She beckoned us with a long hooked forefinger, white as a leper's: "Come closer . . . closer . . . until I can see the whites of your eyes . . . Then we can fire away at one another more effectively . . ."

I would have hung back, but Robin had hold of my wrist and pushed me along ahead of him until we stood a couple of paces in front of her—near enough for her to catch hold of me if she'd have leant forward suddenly.

Robin took the collecting tin from under his coat and jangled it: we'd put a few ha-pence in before we set out so it would make a good noise: "Spare a penny for the old guy, lady."

"So I'm to stand and deliver, am I? My money or my life? Perhaps both, Master Death, eh?" She took up a horrible black net bag from her lap—like the nets they peg out in a rabbit warren when they're ferreting, only darker and more of it—and her fingers worked at the mouth of it in a kind of weaving way, like long white worms, a kind of maggoty movement in the blackness. "But you must unmask first—or you'll be getting money under false pretences. Now which shall I choose to unmask first?" She pointed a wriggling white finger at us, *"Eenie, meenie, mina mo! Catch a nigger by his toe . . ."* The finger jabbed stiff, pointed at my heart. "Take it off," she ordered. "Remove that mask, child, and—"

I fumbled with my spectacles: it was as if I were hypnotised into it. I took them off. I took off my hat, and at the last I pulled off the nigger mask.

"And it's just as I fancied," she added. "A whey-faced boy. His mask is black, but oh, his soul is white. A pudding face and a lily liver." Her finger crooked back like a snake, and struck out at Robin's chest. "Next boy!" she said.

I could hear Robin's troubled breathing as he pulled off his hat and eased the mask elastic over his head. "It's worth a copper, missus," he said, and I'd never heard his tone so uneasy.

"Copper?" she said. "And it's a bright, new-minted copper, boy, too! Master Death is pink as Cupid, and his head is a torch brazier to warm the hands at; even *my* hands might thaw with that head for a muff . . ." It was as if she were speaking to herself; but suddenly she leant forward and stretched out her hands. "Give me the masks," she said, "and I'll show you a trick, shall I? . . . An optical illusion, if you like long words."

She'd snatched them from us before we knew what she would be at, and was sitting back with the masks caught like moths in a spider's web among that black stuff she was wearing. Her fingers worked again at the bag in her lap, and she took out a couple of pennies. They were black Victorian pennies, and she handed us over one apiece. Mine was ice cold, and the "tails" side was green with a kind of mould like verdigris.

"Now place them on my eyes," she said. "Press them in hard. You needn't be afraid of hurting me." Neither of us moved.

"Give them to *me* then." We surrendered the pennies in silence, and she pressed them into her eyes. In that pale thin face they looked like sockets from which the eyes had fallen in dust. "And now the masks . . ."

She covered her face first with my nigger mask, and it was as though her face had fallen off leaving only darkness and nothing; or like the

78

black cloth they cover a murderer's face with on the trapdoor—I'd nightmares after seeing that once in a slot machine in Blackpool. It made me shiver to see her—though I couldn't see her well, my glasses being still in my fingers since I'd taken off the mask.

She picked up Robin's mask next and put it on over mine—and the blackness in the sockets where the pennies were was like . . . well, though the words came to me years later, it was them I was groping for . . . like *eternal night*, sir.

"And now, children," her voice sounded muffled and thinner than ever under the masks, "find the pennies."

"Go on, Friar Tuck," said Robin. "Don't be a fraidy custard. Don't stand there like a dumb loony. The lady wants you to take off the mask."

Very gingerly I reached out my hand to the mask: it seemed to fall off of its own accord into my fingers. I stood and stared fuzzily while Robin, encouraged by my success, reached out for the second mask.

Two masks came away in his hands—and dropped on to the lady's knees. I heard Robin whimpering, and felt my throat go withered at what I looked at. One of the masks that lay upwards on her lap was the lady's face . . . the thin high-cheekboned face with the red line of the mouth now looked up at me vacantly from her knees.

I thought it was something to do with my eyesight being weak; and automatically as it were I fumbled on the mask I was holding and the glasses on top of it.

Then I began whimpering, too. The lady had a different face—a dreadful scarred sunken thing with the flesh of the nose eaten with decay.

"Stop blubbering!" Her voice was sharp and cold as ever. "Why shouldn't I wear masks, too—on the Fifth of November? Did I blubber and cry when two little monsters came up to me out of the fog? You'd think if this was my face I had had some terrible accident, wouldn't you? Or perhaps I was marked with a fearful disease, eh? But you can stop whimpering: it's only a mask. And if it wasn't—well, accidents on this dark earth are all part of a Design, you know— and that disease, well it's an epidemic as common as the cold, isn't it, Master Death?"

We heard the words, but the meaning didn't come till later, years later: I'm not sure I've caught it, the meaning that is, even now. But the sound of her voice seemed to lull us into a kind of trance. We'd stopped wailing—but I heard somebody's teeth chattering, and couldn't be sure they weren't my own.

"You've not found the pennies yet. Now, who's going to take *this* mask off? . . . *Eenie, meenie, mina mo. Catch a . . .*" She stopped, and though the black empty eyes showed no sign of life, one *knew* that she was looking at someone else, someone standing a little behind us. It may have been the lift of that hideous mask—something, a new alertness in the thin body perhaps—that made me glance over my shoulder. "Another boy?" she said. "Another dear little child to watch my trick with the pennies. Well, I've quite an audience now: a flock, a congregation. Come nearer, child."

At first I thought he was wearing a mask, too, this newcomer—his face was so white and his eyes stared so. He was a boy a year or two younger than Robin and me; fair hair he had and neatly brushed, and a neat grey overcoat and grey stockings. He had in one hand a linen bag which held his dancing pumps, for you could see a patent-leather toe stuck out at the top. He had been coming back from a dancing class or some kid's party across the Town Fields. Perhaps he lived in one of the big villas whose lights we'd seen winking back there beyond the foggy garden trees.

He was not the kind of boy Robin or I cared for at ordinary times; if we'd met him alone we'd have teased him, thrown his shiny shoes among the mangel-wurzels and told him to get his hands dirty looking for them. "Little Lord Fauntleroy?" we'd have mocked at him (there wasn't "cissy" in the dictionary in those days), and pushed him about, rubbed mud in his hair, had our bit of fun out of him. But now . . . I can't speak for Robin, but for myself I was glad of his coming, and pitiful, too. I wanted to warn him; I wanted to say: "Run, lad, run as fast as you can before she pins you here as she's pinned me and my friend. Run and bring help!" But all I could get out was a croaking "Hallo, kid." I tried to sound friendly out of gratitude that we were no longer alone.

Even scared as he was, there was a stuck-up air about that little fellow. Oh, it was courage he had all right. "Is she frightening you?" he asked, and a voice he had like my mother used to call "real class." "I've seen her here once or twice before." And he added so low she shouldn't, not with *ordinary* ears, have caught it: "I think perhaps she's a patient that's been released from some . . . some home: an asylum, you know . . . What's that she's wearing on her face?"

"A mask!" the thin muffled voice took him up. "And who is going to remove it and find the pennies . . . *Who shall we have to fetch it away?* . . . Not *you*, my little fair-spoken dancing partner? . . . No one? Then I shall be forced to take it off myself . . ."

Her long writhing fingers went up to her face, and she peeled off that sunken horror—and revealed Robin's mask, the skull-face sitting there bonily as before.

Now there was a trick I could appreciate. She

must have slipped Robin's mask out of his fingers while she talked, and fitted it on under the other without our noticing anything. This was quite a trick, I thought—and I lost something of my . . . my discomfort, thinking how she'd done it. It would have needed a real conjurer's sleight of hand to have slipped it away and under, the way she must have done . . .

"She's diddled you, Robin," I said. "She's won your mask back again, look."

And I wasn't prepared for what happened next. Robin screamed: he just stood and screamed, because the words wouldn't come.

"Robin, whatever's up?" I cried, all over gooseflesh. "What's come over you, Robin?"

He stopped yelling then. He shuddered, and when he spoke it was in a tired voice, not like himself.

"*You're* wearing my mask, Fred. You took it off her first time and put it on your face. You've got it on now—and your specs sitting over it."

I put my hand up to the mask, and before I'd taken it off to look I knew that what Robin had said was the truth. I felt I could drop: I was past screaming.

"So we have four masks," the old horror cut in, "and the question is still—where are the pennies? Are the wages of sin under *this*?" She tapped the hard frontal bone with her fingernail.

"What do *you* think, Master Wheyface Death? Or is there a fifth mask, eh Redbreast? Or nothing perhaps—nothing at all, my little Nijinsky? Well, we've got to find out—some day, haven't we? So who is going to take the fourth mask off, my pretty dears? . . . Shall I pick a volunteer? Eh?"

The long crooked finger uncoiled again from her bosom and she wriggled it at us in turn and began again that fearful singsong—a familiar kid's jingle, but intoned as if it were some black litany in that chill high voice of hers:

> *Eenie, meenie, mina mo!*
> *Catch a nigger by his toe,*
> *If he squeals let him go,*
> *Eenie . . . meenie . . . mina . . . Mo!*

The finger was still and pointed at my heart—and I was moving forward with a dragging sickness on me like despair. It was like the crisis of nightmare, and I was stretching forward my hand to that bony horror under the black straw bonnet when my wrist was seized, and a voice called in my ear—over thousands of light-years it seemed: "No, no . . . Leave her. She's mad darkness. Come away."

It was the fair-haired kid, him with the dancing-pumps. "My people live only a little way down the path there. Come back with me. You're not well. They can telephone . . ."

He was interrupted by that odious thin and ice-edged voice—sharp now as a claw:

"Then if no one will assist me I shall have to take off the fourth mask *all* by myself . . ."

Her hands went up to the thing that wasn't a face and . . . and Robin and I squealed. We hollered as if the hearts were being pulled out between our ribs. And it was as if that screaming released the trance in which we had been held.

"If he squeals let him go . . ." Oh yes, we squealed all right, and went on squealing as we raced away under the sputtering gas lamps. Terror made me glance round to see if she was following. No—she sat there still as a pillar, and there was something white in her hands that maybe was a mask. The fair kid was standing as still in front of her; he hadn't moved or made a single cry. I turned my head away and pounded on, screaming for help.

It was quite dark now, and the fog had grown thicker. Robin had left me behind; but I came across him in a few moments, crouched under an ivy-topped wall and retching.

When we had breath back to speak, Robin sobbed:

"Who *was* she? Who, in mercy's name, was she, Fred?"

"The kid thought she'd escaped from . . . from somewhere," I said.

"Did he run off, too? . . . Did he get away?"

"He stayed," I said. "He stayed to see what was under that bone . . . to look at the Fifth Mask, Robin."

"We shouldn't have left him," said Robin, "not with *her* . . . not alone as he was."

"He could have run off same as we."

"She'd mesmerised him, that's what—same as she done to us."

"He was a plucky kid . . ." I don't know why I used the past tense: the words seemed to be given to me. "I think he stayed because he wanted to see . . . whether she *was* anything at all, living I mean."

"He wanted to *see* . . .?" cried Robin. "Oh no, not that. He'd have run off if he could."

"Perhaps it's been us imagining things, Robin. She couldn't have *harmed* us, when you come to think of it. She was a bit cracked, that's all—but not sufficient to be put away."

Robin was always the leader of our gang at school—and now it was the old Robin Hood that was coming to life in him again.

"We shouldn't have left him with her, Fred. It wasn't right. Not after the way he spoke up when you were going to . . . going to—"

"I know," I said, and shivered. "I know what I was going to do."

"We'll have to go back there and . . . and call him, Friar."

"Catch me going back there, Robin—not if

wild horses was to come and fetch me . . ." And I shivered again because the words raised a picture before my mind's eye of the kind of wild horses that might be sent to fetch me—glossy, tar-black stallions with fire-coal eyes, and smoky manes, and black ostrich plumes tossing from their heads—funeral horses and the glass hearse rattling behind.

"You got to," said Robin. "It's an order; and I'm going with you, anyway . . ."

"No," I said. "I'm sick. *He* saw I was sick. If she speaks to me again I'll . . . I couldn't bear it, Robin . . . You'll have to go yourself. I'll wait here for you to . . . to come back with him."

"You wouldn't like to be left alone . . . in the dark, Fred. And *I'm* going back . . ."

I ran after him. I implored him not to go. I wept and swore, but he kept on.

The seat lay on the outer edge of a pool of gaslight. We approached cautiously—but from fifteen yards away you could see there was nothing there.

"It's all right," I said. "She's gone. We can turn back, *please*, Robin."

"There's something huddled up on the path, far corner of the seat, look. Here, let me get my flashlight."

"It's only a Guy Fawkes someone's set there," I whispered. "Let's turn back, Robin; let's get home."

"It's moving," said Robin. "It's moving on hands and knees. It's dragging something that looks like a mask . . . something white." The thing moved painfully slowly towards the ring of the lamplight, and as it moved it moaned like an animal.

"It's *her*," I cried. "It's her coming for us." But even as I was shouting it I knew that I lied, that it wasn't her and that I was both a coward and a traitor. But in the same moment Robin's nerve had broken again—and it was with a kind of savage desolation in my heart I saw him waver, turn and run back along the path. I followed in panic of being left behind—but by the time we'd pulled up it was of myself that I was most afraid, and of the thing I'd done. Robin had known, too, what that thing was that crept towards the light: I could tell it in his face that was set like a mask.

We said nothing. The Fifth had begun in earnest. There were heavy thuds through the fog, and here and there in the gardens the red flicker and glow of a bonfire. Once a rocket broke right overhead and threw out a handful of drifting blue stars.

We never spoke of that night again—not aloud: the talking was *inside* for each of us, I suppose, over and over, for ever and ever. But I

did hear a scrap of talk between my parents a
night or two later when they thought I was
sleeping.

"Weak heart, poor kid," my father was saying.
"He'd overstrained it the same afternoon, dancing. And there was something that had given him
a shock—a banger, I shouldn't wonder. They
found him on the doorstep. He'd crept there to
die. And that was a peculiar thing, Martha—he
was clutching a Fawkes Day mask when they
found him: shaped like a sleeping child, it was."

"Poor little boy—*dreadful!*" said my mother.
"Why, it might have been our Fred. And fancy
cremating him—a little boy: it's not as if they
couldn't afford a proper funeral."

I was biting my pillow to keep in the sobs that
were shaking me in the dark. Before my parents
were asleep, it was wet whichever way I turned
it.

It may have been coincidence. After all, I
wasn't to *know* it was the same boy. And I didn't
tell Robin what I'd heard either; but I believe he
knew already.

I've only had two real friends in my life—
barring my parents—and both of them's . . .
gone. They know what was under the masks: if
there was *anything*, I mean.

You've been kind listening, sir. It would be an

added kindness if you'd come with me to the door . . . and look out and tell me if those kids in the masks have gone . . . No, that'll be all right, sir . . . It's only a step across the road and down the moving stairs. There's regular trains to Kensal Green.

THE HORROR AT CHILTON CASTLE

Joseph Payne Brennan

The influence of H. P. Lovecraft hovered over *Weird Tales* for most of that magazine's life, but there was another *Weird Tales* style almost as distinctive, the careful spare writing best exemplified by Manly Wade Wellman and Carl Jacobi. In the last years of the magazine Joseph Payne Brennan's "Slime" made it clear that the style had another considerable exponent, and the promise of that noted tale has been kept by many Brennan yarns over the years. Here is one of his finest, to prove what a master of the art can do with a traditional theme.

I HAD DECIDED to spend a leisurely summer in Europe, concentrating, if at all, on genealogical research. I went first to Ireland, journeying to Kilkenny where I unearthed a mine of legend and authentic lore concerning my remote Irish ancestors, the O'Branonains, chiefs of Ui Duach in the ancient kingdom of Ossory. The Brennans (as the name was later spelled) lost their estates in the British confiscation under Thomas Wentworth, Earl of Strafford. The thieving Earl, I am happy to report, was subsequently beheaded in the Tower.

From Kilkenny I traveled to London and then to Chesterfield in search of maternal ancestors, the Holborns, Wilkersons, Searles, etc. Incomplete and fragmentary records left many great gaps, but my efforts were moderately successful and at length I decided to go further north and visit the vicinity of Chilton Castle, seat of Robert Chilton-Payne, the twelfth Earl of Chilton. My relationship to the Chilton-Paynes was a most distant one, and yet there existed a tenuous thread of past connection and I thought it would amuse me to glimpse the castle.

Arriving in Wexwold, the tiny village near the castle, late in the afternoon, I engaged a room at the Inn of the Red Goose—the only one there was—unpacked and went down for a simple meal consisting of a small loaf, cheese, and ale.

By the time I finished this stark and yet satisfying repast, darkness had set in, and with it came wind and rain.

I resigned myself to an evening at the inn. There was ale enough, and I was in no hurry to go anywhere.

After writing a few letters, I went down and ordered a pint of ale. The taproom was almost deserted; the bartender, a stout gentleman who seemed forever on the point of falling asleep, was pleasant but taciturn. At length I fell to musing on the strange and frightening legend of Chilton Castle.

There were variations of the legend. Without doubt the original tale had been embroidered down through the centuries, but the essential outline of the story concerned a secret room somewhere in the castle. It was said that this room contained a terrifying spectacle which the Chilton-Paynes were obliged to keep hidden from the world.

Only three persons were ever permitted to enter the room: the presiding Earl of Chilton, the Earl's male heir, and one other person designated by the Earl. Ordinarily this person was the Factor of Chilton Castle. The room was entered only once in a generation; within three days after the male heir came of age, he was conducted to the secret room by the Earl and the Factor. The room was then sealed and never opened again until the heir conducted his own son to the grisly chamber.

According to the legend, the heir was never the same person again after entering the room. Invariably he would become somber and withdrawn; his countenance would acquire a brooding, apprehensive expression which nothing could long dispel. One of the earlier earls of Chilton had gone completely mad and hurled himself from the turrets of the castle.

Speculation about the contents of the secret room had continued for centuries. One version of the tale described the panic-stricken flight of the Gowers with armed enemies hot on their flagging heels. Although there had been bad blood between the Chilton-Paynes and the Gowers, in their desperation the Gowers begged for refuge at Chilton Castle. The Earl gave them entry, conducted them to a hidden room and left with a promise that they would be shielded from their pursuers. The Earl kept his promise; the Gowers' enemies were turned away from the Castle, their murderous plans unconsummated. The Earl, however, simply left the Gowers in the locked room to starve to death. The chamber was not opened until thirty years later when the Earl's son finally broke the seal. A fearful sight met his eyes. The Gowers had starved to death slowly, and at the last, judging by the appearance of the mingled skeletons, had turned to cannibalism.

Another version of the legend indicated that the secret room had been used by medieval earls as a torture chamber. It was said that the ingenious instruments of pain were yet in the room and that these lethal apparatuses still clutched the pitiful remains of their final victims, twisted fearfully in their last agonies.

A third version mentioned one of the female ancestors of the Chilton-Paynes, Lady Susan Glanville, who had reputedly made a pact with the Devil. She had been condemned as a witch but had somehow managed to escape the stake. The date and even the manner of her death were unknown, but in some vague way the secret room was supposed to be connected with it.

As I speculated on these different versions of

the gruesome legend, the storm increased in intensity. Rain drummed steadily against the leaded windows of the inn, and now I could occasionally hear the distant mutter of thunder.

Glancing at the rain-streaked panes, I shrugged and ordered another pint of ale.

I had the fresh tankard halfway to my lips when the taproom door burst open, letting in a blast of wind and rain. The door was shut, and a tall figure muffled to the ears in a dripping greatcoat moved to the bar. Removing his cap, he ordered brandy.

Having nothing better to do, I observed him closely. He looked about seventy, grizzled and weatherworn, but wiry, with an appearance of toughness and determination. He was frowning as if absorbed in thinking through some unpleasant problem, yet his cold blue eyes inspected me keenly for a brief but deliberate interval.

I could not place him in a tidy niche. He might be a local farmer, and yet I did not think that he was. He had a vague aura of authority. Though his clothes were certainly plain, they were, I thought, somewhat better in cut and quality than those of the area countrymen whom I had observed.

A trivial incident opened a conversation between us. An unusually sharp crack of thunder made him turn toward the window. As he did so, he accidentally brushed his wet cap onto the floor. I retrieved it for him; he thanked me; and then we exchanged commonplace remarks about the weather.

I had an intuitive feeling that although he was a normally reticent individual, he was presently wrestling with some severe problem which made him want to hear a human voice. Realizing there was always the possibility that my intuition might have for once failed me, I nevertheless babbled on about my trip, about my genealogical researches in Kilkenny, London, and Chesterfield, and finally about my distant relationship to the Chilton-Paynes and my desire to get a good look at Chilton Castle.

Suddenly I found that he was gazing at me with an expression which, if not fierce, was disturbingly intense. An awkward silence ensued. I coughed, wondering uneasily what I had said to make those cold blue eyes stare at me so fixedly.

At length he became aware of my growing embarrassment. "You must excuse me for staring," he apologized, "but something you said . . ." He hesitated. "Could we perhaps take that table?" He nodded toward a small table which sat half in shadow in the far corner of the room.

I agreed, mystified but curious, and we took our drinks to the secluded table.

He sat frowning for a minute as if uncertain how to begin. Finally he introduced himself as William Cowath. I gave him my name, and still he hesitated. At length he took a swallow of brandy and then looked straight at me. "I am," he stated, "the Factor at Chilton Castle."

I surveyed him with surprise and renewed interest. "What an agreeable coincidence!" I exclaimed. "Then perhaps tomorrow you could arrange for me to have a look at the castle?"

He seemed scarcely to hear me. "Yes, yes, of course," he replied absently.

Puzzled and a bit irritated by his air of detachment, I remained silent.

He took a deep breath and then spoke rapidly, running some of his words together. "Robert Chilton-Payne, the Twelfth Earl of Chilton, was buried in the family vaults one week ago. Frederick, the young heir and now Thirteenth Earl, came of age just three days ago. Tonight it is imperative that he be conducted to the secret chamber!"

I gaped at him in incredulous amazement. For a moment I had an idea that he had somehow heard of my interest in Chilton Castle and was merely "pulling my leg" for amusement in the belief that I was the greenest of gullible tourists.

But there could be no mistaking his deadly seriousness. There was not the faintest suspicion of humor in his eyes.

I groped for words. "It seems so strange—so unbelievable! Just before you arrived, I had been thinking about the various legends connected with the secret room."

His cold eyes held my own. "It is not legend that confronts us; it is fact."

A thrill of fear and excitement ran through me. "You are going there—tonight?"

He nodded. "Tonight. Myself, the young Earl —and one other."

I stared at him.

"Ordinarily," he continued, "the Earl himself would accompany us. That is the custom. But he is dead. Shortly before he passed away, he instructed me to select someone to go with the young Earl and myself. That person must be male—and preferably of the blood."

I took a deep drink of ale and said not a word.

He continued. "Besides the young Earl, there is no one at the Castle save his elderly mother, Lady Beatrice Chilton, and an ailing aunt."

"Who could the Earl have had in mind?" I inquired cautiously.

The Factor frowned. "There are some distant male cousins residing in the country. I have an idea he thought at least one of them might appear for the obsequies. But not one of them did."

"That was most unfortunate!" I observed.

"Extremely unfortunate. And I am therefore asking you, as one of the blood, to accompany the young Earl and myself to the secret room tonight!"

I gulped like a bumpkin. Lightning flashed against the windows, and I could hear rain swishing along the stones outside. When feathers of ice stopped fluttering in my stomach, I managed a reply.

"But I—that is—my relationship is so very remote! I am 'of the blood' only by courtesy, you might say! The strain in me is so very diluted!"

He shrugged. "You bear the name. And you possess at least a few drops of the Payne blood. Under the present urgent circumstances, no more is necessary. I am sure that Earl Robert would agree with me, could he still speak. You will come?"

There was no escaping the intensity, the pressure, of those cold blue eyes. They seemed to follow my mind about as it groped for further excuses.

Finally, inevitably it seemed, I agreed. A feeling grew in me that the meeting had been preordained, that, somehow, I had always been destined to visit the secret chamber in Chilton Castle.

We finished our drinks, and I went up to my room for rainwear. When I descended, suitably attired, the obese bartender was snoring on his stool in spite of savage crashes of thunder which had now become almost incessant. I envied him as I left the cozy room with William Cowath.

Once outside, my guide informed me that we would have to go afoot to the castle. He had purposely walked down to the inn, he explained, in order that he might have time and solitude to straighten out in his own mind the things which he would have to do.

The sheets of heavy rain, the strong wind, and the roar of thunder made conversation difficult. I walked Indian-fashion behind the Factor, who took enormous strides and appeared to know every inch of the way in spite of the darkness.

We walked only a short distance down the village street and then struck into a side road which very soon dwindled to a footpath made slippery and treacherous by the driving rain.

Abruptly the path began to ascend; the footing became more precarious. It was at once necessary to concentrate all one's attention on one's feet. Fortunately, the flashes of lightning were frequent.

It seemed to me that we had been walking for an hour—actually, I suppose, it was only a few minutes—when the Factor finally stopped.

I found myself standing beside him on a flat rocky plateau. He pointed up an incline which rose before us. "Chilton Castle," he said.

For a moment I saw nothing in the unrelieved darkness. Then the lightning flashed.

Beyond high battlemented walls, fissured with age, I glimpsed a great square Norman castle. Four rectangular corner towers were pierced by narrow window apertures which looked like evil slitted eyes. The huge weathered pile was half covered by a mantle of ivy more black than green.

"It looks incredibly old!" I commented.

William Cowath nodded. "It was begun in 1122 by Henry de Montargis." Without another word he started up the incline.

As we approached the castle wall, the storm grew worse. The slanting rain and powerful wind now made speech impossible. We bent our heads and staggered upward.

When the wall finally loomed in front of us, I was amazed at its height and thickness. It had been constructed, obviously, to withstand the best siege guns and battering rams which its early enemies could bring to bear on it.

As we crossed a massive timbered drawbridge, I peered down into the black ditch of a moat, but I could not be sure whether there was water in it. A low arched gateway gave access through the wall to an inner cobblestoned courtyard. This courtyard was entirely empty save for rivulets of rushing water.

Crossing the cobblestones with swift strides,

the Factor led me to another arched gateway in yet another wall. Inside was a second smaller yard and beyond spread the ivy-clutched base of the ancient keep itself.

Traversing a darkened stone-flagged passage, we found ourselves facing a ponderous door, age-blackened oak reinforced with pitted bands of iron. The Factor flung open this door, and there before us was the great hall of the castle.

Four long hand-hewn tables with their accompanying benches stretched almost the entire length of the hall. Metal torch brackets, stained with age, were affixed to sculptured stone columns which supported the roof. Ranged around the walls were suits of armor, heraldic shields, halberds, pikes, and banners—the accumulated trophies and prizes of bloody centuries when each castle was almost a kingdom unto itself. In flickering candlelight, which appeared to be the only illumination, the grim array was eerily impressive.

William Cowath waved a hand. "The holders of Chilton lived by the sword for many centuries."

Walking the length of the great hall, he entered another dim passageway. I followed silently.

As we strode along, he spoke in a subdued voice. "Frederick, the young heir, does not enjoy robust health. The shock of his father's death was severe—and he dreads tonight's ordeal which he knows must come."

Stopping before a wooden door embellished with carved fleurs-de-lis and metal scrollwork, he gave me a shadowed, enigmatic glance and then knocked.

Someone inquired who was there and he identified himself. Presently a heavy bolt was lifted. The door opened.

If the Chilton-Paynes had been stubborn fighters in their day, the warrior blood appeared to have become considerably diluted in the veins of Frederick, the young heir and now Thirteenth Earl. I saw before me a thin, pale young man whose dark, sunken eyes looked haunted and fearful. His dress was both theatrical and anachronistic: a dark green velvet coat and trousers, a green satin waistband, flounces of white lace at neck and wrists.

He beckoned us in, as if with reluctance, and closed the door. The walls of the small room were entirely covered with tapestries depicting the hunt or medieval battle scenes. Drafts of air from a window or other aperture made them undulate constantly; they seemed to have a disturbing life of their own. In one corner of the room there was an antique canopy bed; in another a large writing table with an agate lamp.

After a brief introduction, which included an explanation of how I came to be accompanying them, the Factor inquired if his Lordship was ready to visit the chamber.

Although he was wan in any case, Earl Frederick's face now lost every last trace of color. He nodded, however, and preceded us into the passage.

William Cowath led the way; the Earl followed him; and I brought up the rear.

At the far end of the passage, the Factor opened the door of a cobwebbed supply room. Here he secured candles, chisels, a pick, and a sledgehammer. After packing these into a leather bag which he slung over one shoulder, he picked up a faggot torch which lay on one of the shelves in the room. He lit this, waiting while it flared into a steady flame. Satisfied with this illumination, he closed the room and beckoned for us to continue after him.

Nearby was a descending spiral of stone steps. Lifting his torch, the Factor started down. We trailed after him wordlessly.

There must have been fifty steps in that long downward spiral. As we descended, the stones became wet and cold; the air, too, grew colder. It was laden with the smell of mold and dampness.

At the bottom of the steps we faced a tunnel, pitch-black and silent.

The Factor raised his torch. "Chilton Castle is Norman but is said to have been reared over a Saxon ruin. It is believed that the passageways in these depths were constructed by the Saxons." He peered, frowning, into the tunnel. "Or by some still earlier folk."

He hesitated briefly, and I thought he was listening. Then, glancing round at us, he proceeded down the passage.

I walked after the Earl, shivering. The dead, icy air seemed to pierce to the pith of my bones. The stones underfoot grew slick with a film of slime. I longed for more light, but there was none save that cast by the flickering, bobbing torch of the Factor.

Partway down the passage he paused, and again I sensed that he was listening. The silence seemed absolute, however, and we went on.

The end of the passage brought us to more descending steps. We went down some fifteen and entered another tunnel which appeared to have been cut out of the solid rock on which the castle had been built. White-crusted nitre clung to the walls. The reek of mold was intense. The icy air was fetid with some other odor which I found peculiarly repellent, though I could not name it.

At last the Factor stopped, lifted his torch and slid the leather bag from his shoulder.

I saw that we stood before a wall made of some kind of building stone. Though damp and stained with nitre, it was obviously of much more recent construction than anything we had previously encountered.

Glancing round at us, William Cowath handed me the torch. "Keep a good hold on it, if you please. I have candles, but—"

Leaving the sentence unfinished, he drew the pick from his sling bag and began an assault on the wall. The barrier was solid enough, but after he had worked a hole in it, he took up the sledgehammer and quicker progress was made. Once I offered to take up the sledge while he held the torch, but he only shook his head and went on with his work of demolition.

All this time the young Earl had not spoken a word. As I looked at his tense white face, I felt sorry for him in spite of my own mounting trepidation.

Abruptly there was silence as the Factor lowered the sledgehammer. I saw that a good two feet of the lower wall remained.

William Cowath bent to inspect it. "Strong enough," he commented cryptically. "I will leave that to build on. We can step over it."

For a full minute he stood looking silently into the blackness beyond. Finally, shouldering his bag, he took the torch from my hand and stepped over the ragged base of the wall. We followed suit.

As I entered that chamber, the fetid odor which I had noticed in the passage seemed to overwhelm us. It washed around us in a nauseating wave, and we all gasped for breath.

The Factor spoke between coughs. "It will subside in a minute or two. Stand near the aperture."

Although the reek remained repellently strong, we could at length breathe more freely.

William Cowath lifted his torch and peered into the black depths of the chamber. Fearfully, I gazed around his shoulder.

There was no sound and at first I could see nothing but nitre-encrusted walls and wet stone floor. Presently, however, in a far corner, just beyond the flickering halo of the faggot torch, I saw two tiny fiery spots of red. I tried to convince myself that they were two red jewels, two rubies, shining in the torchlight.

But I knew at once—I *felt* at once—what they were. They were two red eyes, and they were watching us with a fierce unwavering stare.

The Factor spoke softly. "Wait here."

He crossed toward the corner, stopped halfway and held out his torch at arm's length. For a moment he was silent. Finally he emitted a long shuddering sigh.

When he spoke again, his voice had changed. It was only a sepulchral whisper. "Come forward," he told us in that strange hollow voice.

I followed Earl Frederick until we stood at either side of the Factor.

When I saw what crouched on a stone bench in that far corner, I felt sure that I would faint. My heart literally stopped beating for perceptible seconds. The blood left my extremities; I reeled with dizziness. I might have cried out, but my throat would not open.

The entity which rested on that stone bench was like something that had crawled up out of hell. Piercing malignant red eyes proclaimed that it had a terrible life, and yet that life sustained itself in a black, shrunken half-mummified body which resembled a disinterred corpse. A few moldy rags clung to the cadaver-like frame. Wisps of white hair sprouted out of its ghastly gray-white skull. A red smear or blotch of some sort covered the wizened slit which served it as a mouth.

It surveyed us with a malignancy which was beyond anything merely human. It was impossible to stare back into those monstrous red eyes. They were so inexpressibly evil, one felt that one's soul would be consumed in the fires of their malevolence.

Glancing aside, I saw that the Factor was now supporting Earl Frederick. The young heir had sagged against him. The Earl stared fixedly at the fearful apparition with terror-glazed eyes. In spite of my own sense of horror, I pitied him.

The Factor sighed again, and then he spoke once more in that low sepulchral voice.

"You see before you," he told us, "Lady Susan Glanville. She was carried into this chamber and fettered to the wall in 1473."

A thrill of horror coursed through me; I felt that we were in the presence of malign forces from the Pit itself.

To me the hideous thing had appeared sexless, but at the sound of its name, the ghastly mockery of a grin contorted the puckered red-smeared mouth.

I noticed now for the first time that the monster actually was secured to the wall. The great double shackles were so blackened with age that I had not noticed them before.

The Factor went on, speaking as if by rote. "Lady Glanville was a maternal ancestor of the Chilton-Paynes. She had commerce with the Devil. She was condemned as a witch but escaped the stake. Finally her own people forcibly overcame her. She was brought in here, fettered, and left to die."

He was silent a moment and then continued. "It was too late. She had already made a pact with the Powers of Darkness. It was an unspeakably evil thing, and it has condemned her issue to a life of torment and nightmare, a lifetime of terror and dread."

He swung his torch toward the blackened red-eyed thing. "She was a beauty once. She hated death. She feared death. And so she finally bartered her own immortal soul—and the bodies of her issue—for eternal earthly life."

I heard his voice as in a nightmare; it seemed to be coming from an infinite distance.

He went on. "The consequences of breaking the pact are too terrible to describe. No descendant of hers has ever dared to do so, once the forfeit is known. And so she has bided here for these nearly five hundred years."

I had thought he was finished, but he resumed. Glancing upward, he lifted his torch toward the roof of that accursed chamber. "This room," he said, "lies directly underneath the family vaults. Upon the death of the male Earl, the body is ostensibly left in the vaults. When the mourners have gone, however, the false bottom of the vault is thrust aside and the body of the Earl is lowered into this room."

Looking up, I saw the square rectangle of a trapdoor above.

The Factor's voice now became barely audible. "Once every generation Lady Glanville feeds—on the corpse of the deceased Earl. It is a provision of that unspeakable pact which cannot be broken."

I knew now—with a sense of horror utterly beyond description—whence came that red smear on the repulsive mouth of the creature before us.

As if to confirm his words, the Factor lowered his torch until its flame illuminated the floor at the foot of the stone bench where the vampiric monster was fettered.

Strewn about the floor were the scattered bones and skull of an adult male, red with fresh blood. And at some distance were other human bones, brown and crumbling with age.

At this point young Earl Frederick began to scream. His shrill hysterical cries filled the chamber. Although the Factor shook him roughly, his terrible shrieks continued, terror-filled, nerve-shaking.

For moments the corpse-like thing on the bench watched him with its frightful red eyes. It uttered a sound finally, a kind of animal squeal which might have been intended as laughter.

Abruptly then, and without any warning, it slid from the bench and lunged toward the young Earl. The blackened shackles which fettered it to the wall permitted it to advance only a yard or two. It was pulled back sharply; yet it lunged again and again, squealing with a kind of hellish glee which stirred the hair on my head.

William Cowath thrust his torch toward the monster, but it continued to lunge at the end of its fetters. The nightmare room resounded with the Earl's screams and the creature's horrible squeals of bestial laughter. I felt that my own mind would give way unless I escaped from that anteroom of hell.

For the first time during an ordeal which would have sent any lesser man fleeing for his life and sanity, the iron control of the Factor appeared to be shaken. He looked beyond the wild lunging thing toward the wall where the fetters were fastened.

I sensed what was in his mind. Would those fastenings hold, after all these centuries of rust and dampness?

On a sudden resolve he reached into an inner pocket and drew out something which glittered in the torchlight. It was a silver crucifix. Striding forward, he thrust it almost into the twisted face of the leaping monstrosity which had once been the ravishing Lady Susan Glanville.

The creature reeled back with an agonized scream which drowned out the cries of the Earl. It cowered on the bench, abruptly silent and motionless, only the pulsating of its wizened mouth and the fires of hatred in its red eyes giving evidence that it still lived.

William Cowath addressed it grimly. "Creature of hell! If ye leave that bench ere we quit this room and seal it once again, I swear that I shall hold this cross against ye!"

The thing's red eyes watched the Factor with an expression of abysmal hatred. They actually appeared to glow with fire. And yet I read in them something else—fear.

I suddenly became aware that silence had descended on that room of the damned. It lasted only a few moments. The Earl had finally stopped screaming, but now came something worse. He began to laugh.

It was only a low chuckle, but it was somehow worse than all his screams. It went on and on, softly, mindlessly.

The Factor turned, beckoning me toward the partially demolished wall. Crossing the room, I climbed out. Behind me the Factor led the young Earl, who shuffled like an old man, chuckling to himself.

There was then what seemed an interminable interval, during which the Factor carried back a sack of mortar and a keg of water which he had previously left somewhere in the tunnel. Working by torchlight, he prepared the cement and proceeded to seal up the chamber, using the same stones which he had displaced.

While the Factor labored, the young Earl sat motionless in the tunnel, chuckling softly.

There was silence from within. Once, only, I heard the thing's fetters clank against stone.

At last the Factor finished and led us back through those nitre-stained passageways and up the icy stairs. The Earl could scarcely ascend; with difficulty the Factor supported him from step to step.

Back in his tapestry-panelled chamber, Earl Frederick sat on his canopy bed and stared at the floor, laughing quietly. Medical tomes to the contrary, I noticed that his black hair had actually turned gray. After persuading him to drink a glass of liquid which I had no doubt contained a heavy dose of sedation, the Factor managed to get him stretched out on the bed.

William Cowath then led me to a nearby bed-chamber. My impulse was to rush from that hellish pile without delay, but the storm still raged and I was by no means sure I could find my way back to the village without a guide.

The Factor shook his head sadly. "I fear his Lordship is doomed to an early death. He was never strong and tonight's events may have deranged his mind—may have weakened him beyond hope of recovery."

I expressed my sympathy and horror. The Factor's cold blue eyes held my own. "It may be," he said, "that in the event of the young Earl's death, you yourself might be considered . . . " He hesitated. "Might be considered," he finally concluded, "as one somewhat in the line of succession."

I wanted to hear no more. I gave him a curt good night, bolted the door after him and tried

—quite unsuccessfully—to salvage a few minutes' sleep.

But sleep would not come. I had feverish visions of that red-eyed thing in the sealed chamber escaping its fetters, breaking through the wall and crawling up those icy, slime-covered stairs. . . .

Even before dawn I softly unbolted my door and like a marauding thief crept shivering through the cold passageways and the great deserted hall of the castle. Crossing the cobbled courtyards and the black moat, I scrambled down the incline toward the village.

Long before noon I was well on my way to London. Luck was with me; the next day I was on a boat bound for the Atlantic run.

I shall never return to England. I intend always to keep Chilton Castle and its permanent occupant at least an ocean away.

THE CLERKS OF DOMESDAY

John Brunner

John Brunner has often dealt with terrors, from the futures of his novels *Quicksand* and the Hugo winner *Stand on Zanzibar* to the ominously inexplicit *Players at the Game of People*. Here is a tale which seems to have proved too grim for other editors, one of the good reasons why I include it here.

He caused to be written . . . how much each man had who was a holder of land . . . and how much money it were worth. So very narrowly he caused it to be searched out that there was not a single hide or a yard of land nor even—it is shame to tell though it seemed to him no shame to do—an ox, nor a cow, nor a swine was left that was not set down in his writing.

—"The Making of Domesday Boke," from *The Anglo-Saxon Chronicle,* A.D. 1085

IF ONLY I'D had the sense to finish him off . . . But I've hated war and violence since I was a kid, and last night, when I saw him lying in the shadows of that crack-walled alley, bleeding among the garbage and the scrabbling rats, I just had to get the hell away from the reality of what I'd done. At least I had the sense to take along the club I'd used to beat him and dump it where the rubbish heaps burn night and day. By now, with luck, it should have charred to nothing.

Later, calmer, I went back, having figured out that there was no alternative to shutting his mouth for good and all, not unless I wanted to spend the balance of my life in jail or an asylum —and of course there was no sign of him. Nor the rest of his gang. They've vanished, the lot of them, like smoke on the wind.

I don't know whether it was they who found him, or someone else, and I can't tell which would be worse. Most likely he wouldn't have talked to the *Guardias Civiles*, even if he could, but I don't stand a cat in hell's chance of hiding from his chums forever, with all the power of the CIA or the Pentagon or whatever it is behind them.

And if it *was* the truth I forced out of him at the end . . .

No, I can't believe that. I mustn't. It was some kind of crazy cover story, maybe hypnotically implanted, so deep the guy wound up being convinced of it himself. They can do that sort of thing nowadays. You read about it all the time.

But there is something that I do believe. You've got to believe it too. You've got to listen to me. For God's sake—and much more for your own—pay attention!

The decision has been made to abolish Europe.

Now I see it down on the page, that looks silly. How else can I express it, though? "Spend" Europe? Closer, maybe; whoever they are who've made the plans will have balanced this against that, so many deaths and so much uninhabitable land on this side against so much more damage on the other, to the point of genocide and deserts. Or should I say "waste" Europe?

I'm sure they wouldn't think of it as waste. More as a necessary price.

This has to be written in scraps and snatches. Every now and then, hearing a noise, I panic, shoving my notebook and pen inside my jacket, and stare around for whoever is coming to get me. But so far I seem to have eluded them. Even so, I move on whenever this happens. I can't help it. There's a limit to the tolerance of even the most indulgent bar owner, and I can't afford more than a soft drink or a cup of coffee, which I have to stretch for hours.

I ought to eat something. Will. Tonight at closing time I'll find a bar where they're throwing out stale bread and leftover tapas. I've done it before. But right now this is more important.

I must get the point across to you. *There is going to be a nuclear war.* It will wipe out Europe but the people who are planning it regard that as incidental. The purpose is, presumably, to write off Russia and China, thereby ridding Mother Earth of godless commies. I've worked it all out.

Now you're going to ask for evidence. I can only say: you can find the proof the same way I did, just by looking. They're everywhere. Depending where you live, some of them may be right on your doorstep. If you travel to any of the famous towns and cities of Europe, you'll see plenty of them provided you keep your eyes peeled. That's how I stumbled on what's happening.

But I haven't yet told you who "they" are, so I'll have to explain.

The first I spotted were in Athens, and they were—or rather, appeared to be—Japanese. That seems to be part of a standard pattern: they always claim to come from a long way away, and generally they look very different from the locals. I suppose it helps to preserve their cover, because everybody expects foreigners to behave in weird and unfamiliar ways. Lord knows I got enough of that when I first arrived in Stockholm, way back when.

(In case you're wondering: yes, I was a draft

dodger. I made for Sweden when things got too disgusting in Vietnam. Right now I wish I was dead over there, free from knowledge of what I've found out since.)

Those Japanese . . . Well, after bumming around this tired old continent for as long as I have, you get to spot the petty differences between one nationality and another. It turns into a kind of private game. You look them over, and you make up little stories about these total strangers and give them invented names, and it all helps to pass the time before the next cheap bus or train is due to leave. People in my position don't have what one would call high-order earning capacity.

Now I've seen plenty of Japanese tourists, from Wales to Turkey, from Finland to Morocco, which are about the limits of my beat. And these weren't right. They behaved in more or less the normal way, but . . . Hell, there's a phrase I need that I last used in college . . . Got it. "Standard deviation"—from statistics, I think. That's what these people had. It wasn't just that some of them acted differently from the norm; you might get a handful of eccentrics in any group. No: all of them were nearly but not quite right for the pattern they were trying to follow, and all of them were askew in exactly the same fashion.

So who said they were trying to follow a

pattern? My best answer is that Japanese tour groups are very standard indeed. The only ones tidier and more conformist tend to come from the socialist countries: less the Hungarians than, for instance, the Romanians and Bulgarians. As for the East Germans—but I'm wandering. Habit, I guess; that's been the pattern of *my* life since I left home.

Later again. I've got to stop packing up and running every time I hear a heavy footfall or the slam of a door. That's bound to look suspicious, and until I set down all I know on paper, I've got to behave as ordinarily as possible. I'm making notes, as though for an article, and that's what I'll say if some curious passerby decides to strike up a conversation.

I hope to heaven nobody does.

Back to those Japanese. I'd been to Greece before, but I'd never seen the Parthenon, and there was a rumor about closing it owing to the wear and tear caused by millions of visitors. So, figuring this might be my only chance of contributing to the damage, I'd hitched the usual lifts and made it to Athens. Not speaking word one of the language, and being too broke to afford maps and guidebooks, I learned what I could about the sights I was seeing by tagging along behind guided tours. The day I hit the Acropolis one guide had a gaggle of Japanese in tow, and she was addressing them in English, which suited me fine.

Then—get this. Now and then, as I moved ahead and fell back so as not to make it too obvious that I was freeloading, I found myself close enough to some of these Japanese to notice that they were speaking English too.

When they said anything, that is. Most of the time they were busy with still and video cameras, like you'd expect. Not until, after a good half hour, I caught on to the peculiar fact that so far I hadn't heard a single one of them say anything *except* in English—and that in low tones, as though afraid this huge and public space might be bugged—not till then did I start to take a closer look.

That was when I pinned down what was oddest about them. You know how people on these tours urge their friends to pose on steps or rocks or inside archways, so they can be photographed against a background which will prove to the folks back home—or maybe themselves —that they really did go where they said they went? Of course you do, and these people were following the same routine.

Only when this bunch took station for a picture they didn't just stand and simper in the usual way. They were—they were too *purposeful* to be convincing. Many of them carried sticks, and at first I thought there must be a hell of a lot of the crippled and purblind in the group. Yet they didn't act handicapped . . . or if they were, it was mentally, not physically. They fidgeted constantly; they looked around, they peered into the viewfinders of their cameras even when they didn't seem to be setting up to take pictures themselves (all of them had cameras, and some had sound recorders too); they made constant notes, either written or whispered to tape; and when called on to be in a photo, although they arranged themselves at carefully chosen spots, they never bothered to compose their faces to make a good impression in the family album.

That's what first alerted me. They didn't seem to care how they looked . . . and their expressions were uniformly tense and anxious, as though they were afraid the heavens might fall on them at any moment. Not in the least what you'd expect of a bunch of holidaymakers having the time of their lives, hmm?

But it wasn't obvious enough to bother the guide, whose main concern was to ensure they rejoined their bus at the foot of the hill before its driver grew bored and wandered off in search of a bar, and their thoroughness was making her urge them to get a move on. At one point I caught her eye and grinned, and she spread her hands as much as to say, "Heaven preserve us!"

Me, though, I was glad they weren't in any

hurry. My curiosity had been piqued—I think that's how you spell it—and, still doing my best to pretend I simply happened to be heading in the same direction at the same time, I passed among the group on the down slope. This gave me a chance to look more closely at their cameras and recorders.

Those weren't quite what I was expecting, either.

Oh, they were like enough—as much like ordinary ones as these people were like ordinary tourists, adequate to pass muster. But there were little differences . . .

Do I have one to show? How I wish I did! For I don't really know how to describe them. It's partly a matter of what they made their users do—if you follow me. Example: one of them would plant his stick on this or that step of the Acropolis, and the photographer would tell him to move it to another. Then he would line up for a low shot where it would give an exact standard of measurement, or after a glance at his watch order it tilted to a careful angle so that it would cast the right shadow at this precise moment of the day . . . It was hot. Did I say I was there in June?

Look, it was less like watching a bunch of holidaymakers than a surveying team with levels and theodolites! And now and again I noticed one of them covertly reaching out to rub something: a statue, a pillar, the side of a wall. Oh, not enough to leave a trace. But every time this happened, I saw the same hand sneak into a pocket, as though to store away some tiny speck of dust.

Souvenirs that small did *not* make tourist-type sense.

Eventually they went their way. Puzzled, I watched their bus depart in a cloud of smoke.

As it turned out, next day I had other things to occupy my mind. My folks were supposed to cable me some money and it didn't arrive until a week later, so I was scuffling for a while. Because of that I forgot about the Japanese—which I guess was how they hoped everybody would react—until a month later, when I found myself in Dubrovnik.

People there mainly go to look over the Lovrjenac Fortress with its five great ugly bastions. Why? I guess because it's old—six, seven centuries, maybe. I majored in history, but I don't approve of war and things to do with war, no matter how long they may endure. That day, though, I was restless, and once again I didn't speak the language, so in search of company I could talk to I headed for where there might be English-speaking tourists.

And found some—not Japanese this time, but American. No talent, though, of the sort I was

hoping for; the coach they arrived in was plas-
tered with stickers announcing that they be-
longed to a Bible-study group on a month-long
trip following pilgrim routes to the Holy Land.
Apparently a lot of ships bound for Palestine set
sail from Dubrovnik, though in those days it had
a different name.

That, candidly, is not my scene. I haven't been
in a church except to look at sculpture, paint-
ings or stained glass since I quit the States. But
they had a good loud guide with plenty of
information to impart in English, so I put on my
usual act and tagged along, eavesdropping.

And what did I suddenly notice?

Right. Here was not your regular run of
overfed midwesterners, with their paunches sagging in testimony to where all those millions of
Big Macs wound up, and their wives panting
along behind, stopping every few meters to
complain about the lack of air-conditioning in
the hotels they'd paid good money for. No more
were there any kids in tow, the way I'd have
expected: teenagers hanging back, giggling at
in-group jokes they didn't want their parents to
overhear, or sullen because they hoped for more
out of "abroad" than boring lectures.

No, these people were all of an age, and
almost gaunt, and—like the Japanese in Athens
—they looked worried. Moreover they behaved
in the same way, carried similar sticks, checked

their watches (why?) before having their pictures taken, and concentrated with something akin to desperation on - their cameras and recorders . . . and once again, when I crept close enough to sneak a look, their gear proved to be not quite like the ordinary kind.

Okay, sure: there had been progress in design. Maybe those Japs had been sporting the very latest equipment; they're so goddamned inventive over there. Maybe these folks, here now, were so well-to-do they could all throw away last year's model of everything and pick up the next version for the trip—though sure as hell they didn't dress as if they were that rich. Maybe it was just that none of them had ever been abroad before and wanted up-to-date cameras to trap all the images along the path the pilgrims took, so someone back home closed a bulk-buying deal and got each of them a new model at a discount to them and a profit to himself.

But there are stores in Stockholm where you can see *the* latest, *the* flashiest, *the* most expensive . . . and there hadn't been anything like what this bunch was carrying in the windows along Kungsgatan last Christmas!

Besides—and this was maybe the oddest thing of all—even if you've never handled a brand-new, top-of-the-range camera or video camera or whatever, you have an impression of what it ought to be like: everything about it finished to a flawless engineering standard, almost as though you could cast jewelry in steel and plastic. What these people were toting struck me as . . . well, sort of second-best, like a Russian copy of a Western car.

So I started to pay serious attention.

The image of a party of surveyors came back to me at once; I hadn't thought of it since Athens, but it was apt. The pictures they were taking weren't just portraits of Mr. X and Mrs. Y in this cute/quaint/historic setting. The people were entirely secondary. And, exactly as before, I noticed some of them scratching, or abrading, the walls of the medieval fort, and pocketing a trace of dust.

Most people of that stamp wouldn't so much as put a dirty hand into a pocket, or a purse, except maybe to feel for a tissue. If they couldn't get to soap and water, at least they'd rub their hands together and blow away the traces. Why should they want to take samples?

That's what they were doing. I was suddenly convinced of it. But why?

Later (I had to move on for fear of attracting attention) and late: it must be nearly sunset. I guess I'll have to sleep rough tonight. I daren't go back to the flea-ridden pad where I've been lodging. Still, it isn't raining, and there are places on the riverbank, if you can stand the stench and the cats. But why the hell am I still in Granada, instead of putting as much distance as possible between me and the scene of the crime? I must be crazy . . .

I guess you already decided that. Bear with me, though. Please, for all our sakes. Just let me tell the rest of what I know.

After Dubrovnik I started searching for other tourist groups behaving in the same way.

No, that's not right. I didn't have to hunt for them, not actively. Once I'd cottoned on, I kept spotting them wherever I went. They were at Naples and Pompeii; they were at Rome, Volterra, Milan, Turin, Genoa, Nice, Cannes, Nîmes, Albi, Carcassonne . . . Oh, I can't remember all the places where I found them. It might be quicker to list the ones where I didn't, if I could think of any.

Little by little I started to notice that they seemed to be in an even greater hurry than before, giving an ever more brusque rebuff to me or anyone else who tried to engage them in friendly chat, making less and less of an attempt to blend in among the regular tourists as they went about making a record of every site far more detailed and precise than I could conceive a reason for . . . *short of an attempt to reconstruct it.*

But I'm getting ahead of myself. Let me tell

you what occurred one windy day at Carcassonne, on that broad grey walk beneath the high
grey battlements where men-at-arms might
march abreast by threes.

This time—so their local guide informed me
—the swarthy members of the tour group were
pretending to hail from Brazil, though as ever
they spoke only English among themselves. By
now they were being positively blatant. Almost at
once I noticed that two of them were carrying
what looked like actual surveying gear, though
of a type I'd never seen before. Still, it didn't take
long to figure out how it must work. One of them
would set against a wall a box-shaped device
containing a miniature parabolic horn, rather
like the bottom half of a windup phonograph,
and his partner—a woman—would hold a sort
of small metal saucer against another wall on
the far side of the vast deformed ring of the
fortifications. Now and then it seemed that the
wind caused an inexact reading, but generally
after a few moments they'd nod to each other
and move on somewhere else.

Reasoning that if they were coming so far into
the open, I might as well do the same, I stood
staring at the man until I made him uncomfort-
able. I don't know what he made of me. Perhaps
he found me threatening, because I haven't
shaved or been to a barbershop in years. As for

clothes, I make do with castoffs that often don't fit properly. I guess I looked, as usual, like a walking rummage sale.

If I disturbed him, though, that was all to the good.

By the ninth or tenth time he'd gone through the drill he was looking annoyed; by the fifteenth his patience was on the brink of exhaustion.

At which point I put on my sunniest smile and pointed at the device he was carrying.

"That's new, isn't it?" I said cheerfully. "How does it work—by ranging an ultrasonic pulse?"

For a second I expected him to break and run, but there were a great many other people around, so he thought better of it.

Curtly, and with an accent I could not quite place, he said, "Yes, more or less."

"And after it bounces off the gadget your friend is carrying, a microcomputer automatically converts delay time into distance?"

"Ah . . ." He looked as though he would rather bite out his tongue than give an honest answer, but he was obliged to maintain his rôle. At length he nodded, and went on, "Now please excuse me, for I am being busy."

"Oh! I thought you were just a tourist!"

His eyes flicked from side to side like an animal's in a trap.

"How interesting!" I went on, to needle him. "I suppose you work for the people who look after the castle, do you? But your guide said you were from Brazil!"

"Yes—yes, is so. All our party is from Brazil."

I'd got him well and truly rattled, so I pushed ahead.

"Why in the world should you want to make a survey of this place?"

Now if he'd been really smart, even at that stage he could still have fobbed me off with a neatly turned excuse. He could for example have claimed that his hobby was making exact plans of ancient buildings, or that he was an artist commissioned to illustrate a history book; anything along those lines. I'd have swallowed such a yarn. Because, you see, by now I was afraid I was getting paranoid, and inclined to believe that I'd just been out of touch too long, either in Sweden or while bumming my way from place to place every summer, talking to almost nobody and despite my best efforts losing touch with new gadgetry and the way it was affecting people's habits.

Instead, he lied outright. He said, "I work for the National Museum in Brasilia, to make scale models for its exhibitions. Next year we shall have one about France. It is important to make ready in good time. It being much expensive, so need be perfect. Please, now I go!" He almost ran to join his companion.

Why did his explanation ring false?

Well, though I can't claim to keep up with the news, sometimes I get hungry for reading matter in my mother tongue. Swedish is kind of a limited language compared to English; even a Swede will tell you so. And I don't speak anything else, even French bar a phrase or two.

But in most of the places I find my way to I can't afford the prices they charge for American and British magazines and newspapers, let alone books, so when the fit comes on I have to make do with other people's leavings. A week or two before I'd come across a copy of the *International Herald Tribune* and devoured it down to the classified ads.

Among the news items I recalled one which said that Brazil was on the verge of bankruptcy, and all nonessential outgoings in foreign currency had been banned.

An expensive display in a museum was essential?

What I next wanted to believe was that this report about the Brazilian financial crisis had been wrong. I swear I'd have settled for that— anything except the conclusion I've been driven to. I went in search of more recent news. A railroad station is a good place to pick up magazines and papers thrown away by people who only bought them to pass the time before a train arrived. This time I didn't have much luck, but I did find a gang of French papers which I scanned in the hope of picking out a word here and there, and I guess anyone can recognize *atomique* and *nucléaire*. Additionally there were maps and diagrams which would have got the point across to a dyslexic. Some sort of brand-new missile had been sent to Europe from the States, and it was supposed to be upsetting the balance of terror.

That, I guess, was the point at which the explanation started to dawn on me, though it was a while before I worked out the details. I stared at those maps, and thought of the places I'd been to and what would happen if the war they depicted actually broke out.

It looked as though Spain might be a little safer than most other countries, and maybe from there I could bum my way into Portugal and . . .

Did I want to stay alive if this kind of thing was on the cards? I still don't know. But I decided I could figure out yes or no on my way. If yes, I'd stow away on a ship for South America and take my chance.

Not that it looked like a very good one.

Which brings me to Granada, late in the evening at a table outside the sort of bar that doesn't sound as though it closes before dawn.

Just so long as my funds hold out, I can go on buying soft drinks—they cost more than wine, but I have to stay sober . . . Hell. I'm wasting paper.

What actually brought me here was a stroke of luck so incredible I don't know whether to regard it as coincidence. I hitched a ride with an old man who turned out to have been born in Poland, but joined the Free Polish Air Force during World War II when he was about eighteen, and spent a long time in Britain, where he learned the creaky English he spoke to me. But after the war he decided he couldn't stand the place and couldn't go home either. On that score I knew how he felt.

So he moved to France because he'd been taught French as a kid, and set up a business that involved him in frequent travel between Paris and the south of Spain: something to do with fruit, I think. And he must have done nicely, because his car was a Mercedes.

He said he stopped for me because once he too was a refugee. I guess I looked sort of pitiable. It was a grey and chilly morning and mist was turning into rain in the foothills of the Pyrenees.

But—he did most of the talking during the hours we spent together—at least he had regained a grudging admiration for the country of his birth. He said, over and over, that he wished he might revisit Warsaw, because he'd read about how after the war the new government set out to rebuild what had been destroyed by the Nazis. He'd seen pictures of places he'd known as a child, bombed or shelled into ruins, and they'd been reconstructed, using the original architects' drawings, so that one could scarcely tell the difference. All this despite the fact that Poland was among the poorest countries in Europe thanks to the devastation war had wrought.

Something began to tick in the back of my mind, like a time bomb, when his words meshed with a fact I'd retained since college days. Once, long ago, someone had set out to catalogue a country. He'd been a conqueror. I knew that much. But which, and when? There'd been so many!

He dropped me off here in Granada. He was going further south, to Málaga, but his descriptions of what had overtaken Poland in World War II had inclined me to despair, and I needed time. I hadn't mentioned to him what had driven me away from France, for I was frankly scared of doing so. Who could contemplate destruction a thousand times worse, and coldly plot to bring it to pass?

Either I must be out of my mind . . . or they must.

* * *

And then, next day—the day before yesterday —at the Alhambra, I found just what I'd run across elsewhere: a tour group acting like surveyors. They were black, but spoke English. The reason for their presence . . .

Cancel that. During the night I'd remembered who the conqueror was who set out to describe a whole country, didn't make it, and nonetheless fooled himself into believing that he had, so that the records compiled by his clerks were called *The Domesday Book*—true and valid till the day of judgment. So change it to: the excuse for their presence was that they were a bunch of Black Muslims looking over those areas of Europe which once were under the sway of Islam, and fell through Christian double-dealing and deceit. Well, some of that is fact though more by now is surely fiction . . .

But I knew the truth. I'd worked it out. I'd settled on the only possible reason why anyone should be spending what must amount to millions of dollars in order to make a permanent record of Western Europe: its monuments, its museums, its buildings, its . . .

No, not so much its art galleries. So much of what they once had to show has already been disposed of to the New World. But things like the Acropolis and the walls of Carcassonne are a mite too big for shipment overseas.

It fits. It all fits. So now I have a name for these

"tourists," busy making records of the old Europe that's going to go smash in World War III so that bits at least of it can be reconstructed afterwards. Maybe you guessed it.

They're the Clerks of Domesday.

I wanted to rush around shouting the bad news. But how the hell could I make anybody listen?

I concluded I'd have to get one of the clerks to admit the truth. First I thought: maybe if I could con somebody into lending me a tape recorder and a rifle mike I might pick up some snatches of unguarded conversation. Then I started to see all the obstacles. I wasn't sure they'd return to the Alhambra tomorrow. Big though it is, there were probably enough of them in the group—over thirty—to cover it in a single day, especially with their equipment. Moreover I hadn't the faintest notion how to get hold of such a mike, and even if I did they were probably too well briefed to let anything slip. The behavior of every group I'd seen indicated a slick, carefully planned operation with a lot of money behind it. Where had they all been recruited, anyway? Maybe there was a clue in that Bible-study tour I'd met at Dubrovnik. Yes, that seemed likely: religious fanatics prepared to bring on Armageddon might gladly volunteer . . . Think of Iran!

143

But I must get one of them to talk, and I must record his confession. I couldn't afford to buy a tape recorder. Perhaps I could steal one?

Me? Who never stole anything more than change out of mom's purse when I was five?

After lying awake half the night, I still hadn't hit on a solution. Blear-eyed, sour-bellied, around seven I dragged myself out of the flophouse I was staying in and went hunting— without much optimism—for the clerks.

They weren't at the Alhambra today. Nor the Generalife, nor the cathedral, nor the royal chapel. From one tourist attraction to another I pounded pavement in the warm air but wan sunlight of the fall, gazing about me till my eyes ached. How did I know what they regarded as essential? Maybe today they'd quit the city for the gypsy caves in the hills nearby, looking for hints about how to survive after all the houses get blown down . . .

Footsore, thirsty, starving, I gave up an hour after sundown and headed back towards the quarter where I'd spent last night, knowing it was cheap. I had a notebook in my pack, and I'd decided it was time for me to set down on paper what I'd worked out about the clerks.

On the way I found one.

My route took me alongside the river, where they dump garbage and the rats and wild cats thrive, up a sloping street lined with little shops in front of which craftsmen sit making and selling marquetry and leather work. No more customers being in view, they were retreating indoors as darkness fell. Partway up, I spotted one belated stranger, a black man in a hurry. I recognized him from the day before: short, thin, and excessively nervous for a Black Muslim— even more than his companions at the Alhambra.

It hadn't occurred to me till then that sometimes they might split up and work alone rather than in a team. After all, it's easier to spot anomalous behavior among twenty or thirty people than in an individual.

I didn't have time to make plans. He was approaching me with his head down, apparently checking that his video camera was in order. I glanced around. Nobody was paying any attention. The craft workers were reentering their brightly lighted homes, calling to their families —doubtless complaining about today's lousy business and asking whether supper was ready yet. Doors were being slammed and locked. Radios and record players uttered a cats' concerto of garbled speech and loud flamenco music.

And just to my left was an alley.

The light was bad, but I judged it was maybe two meters wide by five or six long. It ended in a blank wall. There was one rough wooden door on either side, but junk and scrap metal were piled so high against both of them that neither could have been opened in years. It was overlooked by four or five upper windows, but they were closed with crude shutters dangling off their hinges and secured with wire. Not a gleam of light showed through any of them.

To judge by the stench, no one had passed this way for a long while, save to use the alley as a toilet.

What I had to do was clear in an instant. I caught the black man's arm and swung him around, clamping my other hand over his mouth, then dragged him into the alley before he could draw breath.

As I forced him to the far end, I trod on something that almost betrayed my footing, thin and round and hard: maybe half a pole from a broken wooden bedstead. I picked it up. It was slimy and filthy, but it would make a weapon.

What I'd have done if my captive had fought back, I can't imagine—or even if he'd screamed loud enough to cut through the music blasting from the nearby houses. But he was so bewildered, he could only cringe. I guess he took me for a thief, for he clutched his video camera tight against his body and hunched over it, eyes staring wide.

On discovering he wasn't apt to offer much resistance, I felt a little better.

I shoved him hard against the far wall. He had

to lean back because there was no footing on the rubbish heaped at its base. Satisfied he was at my mercy, I said, "You don't make records of this kind of thing, do you? You're not planning to reconstruct stinking alleys like this one!"

And he fainted. Fainted clean away.

That was something I hadn't bargained for. Folding at the waist, he sank on the pile of muck. My automatic assumption was that he was faking, so I prodded his midriff with my club, hard enough to make him cry out. He stayed limp.

I tucked my impromptu club under my arm and seized his video camera, dragging its strap from around his neck. Frantically I tried to figure out how it worked—but I couldn't. My worst fears were being confirmed. This gear *was* disguised, doubtless by the cleverest designers in the world, so as to look like what it wasn't . . .

Well, that was evidence of a sort. Hanging it on a handy nail, I turned my attention back to the little guy, who was stirring and starting to moan. Tapping him under the chin with my club, I told him to get up.

Clumsily, like a far-gone drunk, he forced himself not exactly upright but back to his feet, leaning his shoulders against the wall. It looked like a safe position, too much off balance for him to attack me.

What did I need to find out first? Obviously,

why what I'd said before had made him pass out. So, in the hope of convincing him that I'd solved the riddle of his equipment, I summoned my harshest voice.

"Back in the real world, are you? Great! Now I want some straight answers from you!"

"What—what did you say?" he whimpered.

"I said you're not recording this kind of filthy alley! You and your kind only plan to reconstruct the monuments—the Alhambra, the Acropolis, Pompeii and Carcassonne!"

He thought that over for a while. Then he shrugged and seemed to gather his wits. Pushing himself away from the wall with one arm, he wiped his forehead with his other sleeve. His accent was far clearer than the Brazilian's.

Not looking at me, he muttered, "I knew we couldn't get away with it. Someone was bound to catch on . . . Ah, you're right: who'd want to reconstruct a squalid hole like this?"

"So you admit it!" I exploded—remembering just in time to keep my voice down.

"Admit what?" He was making a valiant recovery, his eyes on the camera I'd taken from him.

"That you and the rest—the ones I've seen in Greece and Yugoslavia and France—you're measuring up the places that won't survive the nuclear war, so they can be copied afterward! *You know it's going to happen!*"

I thought for a moment he was about to deny it, and took a fresh grip on my club. Instead, evading my gaze, he let his shoulders slump.

"I knew we couldn't get away with it," he repeated.

"I should goddamned well think not! Christ, if there's anything I can do to stop you! How can you talk so calmly about the greatest crime in all of history?"

And broke off, because he reacted wrong. I was half-expecting him to make a break for it. On the contrary: that was when he said the thing I can't believe.

"Well"—with a sigh—"it all happened too long ago for it to be worth blaming anybody."

"What?"

"Oh yes. More than two hundred years. But, please, you must accept: we're gambling our own lives by being here. We may not get back. If not, we're doomed the same as you."

My head swam. In that moment he could have pushed past me and yelled for help, and called the *Guardias* to arrest me as a mugger. Maybe he was too weak. I don't know and don't care. All I could—all I can—think of is that dull sad voice, echoing between the jag-cracked walls. It rang and rang around my head as well, and drove me mad.

Because I knew (and know) this was a lie. I'd

worked it all out. He and his colleagues had been told about the nuclear war. They were conniving at it. They weren't behaving like decent civilized people, turning their backs and saying, "I won't have any part of it!" Oh no! They'd sold out! In full awareness that the plan had been confirmed, that there was going to be an unprovoked attack with the vilest weapons yet invented, they were lending their services and talents to a hateful scheme. Where would our ancient relics be rebuilt as fakes? In some colossal future Disneyland? "Here's Trajan's Column!"—would they say, the guides in some safe unpolluted refuge underground? "Look over there and note the Elgin Marbles, but don't touch! And that's the Mona Lisa, and the Venus di Milo is right next to it; don't touch! And there's a hologram of how the Chartres Rose Window used to look! So who cares that there isn't a real Europe any more? This place is just as good and maybe better! Don't contradict! It has sanitized toilets, and air-conditioning as well!"

A world built on the bones of you and me . . .

That was what first made me hit him. I cut his scalp, and blood ran down and caught the glint of distant lights across the river.

He couldn't believe it, any more than I could. Something dark and terrible had taken possession of me. I needed to hear the truth, do you understand? And I knew what he said had to be a lie! So I hit him again, across the face and in the belly, and he fell on his knees, babbling.

I said, "I'll go on doing this until you confess!"

"But you know the truth already!" he moaned, blood flowing from his mouth and nose. "You know what we're doing—told me so!"

"Yes, you've sold your souls to the mass murderers who plan to launch a war and wipe out Europe!"

"No, no, no!"—as he crawled around on the pavement, snivelling. "We hate our ancestors now, we despise them! It's true they did this dreadful thing, but we've spent two centuries in trying to make amends!"

I said, "You're mad as well as lying."

"No, believe me!" he implored, striving to raise himself. "They did do what you say, but so long ago! For generations we have starved and frozen and suffered, and now we find the way to make our penance!"

"You expect me to swallow that load of bullshit? Next you'll be telling me you've sent people to wave their cameras around in ancient Rome!"

"No, of course! We can only reach this herenow, where traces of our interference are bound to be wiped out!"

"So you know when they plan to start the war! Tell me!"

"Most we can say is: any day! All the records were destroyed, and at the distance of so many years—"

I hit him again. Moaning, he tried to embrace my legs, imploring mercy. I was in no mood to show him any.

"You've got to do better than that!" I said, kicking him away. "Someone's behind this caper, and spending millions to finance it! Why does all your gear look so shoddy when it's really ultramodern?"

"Not to attract attention!"

"It attracted my attention, didn't it? Try again!"

I pantomimed another blow, and he fell back against the wall with his eyes shut.

"Best we can do," he mumbled. "You squandered so much! There's little left for us—oil gone, most coal, purest ore of metal—"

I hit him again, for real, and felt teeth break loose.

"No good!" he whispered. "No point! Impossible to change anything before time-travel, and that took us two hundred years!"

I called him a son of a bitch and hit him on the head, harder than ever. He tumbled sideways. Nonetheless, lying in a welter of blood that looked black in the gloom, he managed one more utterance.

"You could have had it more cheaply than

weapons. It's simple once you grasp the principle. But then, I guess, you would have fought a war with it. Then nobody like us could come and try to save your relics."

Save? *Save?* This bastard in the pay of the filthiest of all criminals was daring to claim he planned to rescue things that were not yet endangered! And if I could spill his secret to the world they never need be!

"Confess!" I howled, and made to strike again.

And checked my club before it landed. He had grown abruptly still: too still. Lax and inanimate, he sprawled in putrid muck.

All my anger leaked away in icy sweat. I let the club fall and felt his wrist for a pulse. Finding one, though it was weak and irregular, I shook him, ordering him to wake up.

He didn't. I rolled him on his back, and he moved like a dummy full of sawdust. When I plucked up enough courage to touch his head, I could feel fragments of bone moving beneath his scalp like bits of shell around a hard-boiled egg. I'd broken his skull . . .

The world rocked about me. I had to lean against the wall while I threw up. But all that came out was a sour liquid scalding to my throat, for I had drunk little and eaten nothing since the morning.

Bit by bit it dawned on me that his companions would come looking for this guy. I forced my weak legs to carry me as far as the mouth of the alley—and remembered the club, which might be smooth enough to reveal my fingerprints, so I went back for it. During those few moments I really must have been insane. Why else did I not take his video camera too?

Maybe because a part of me was hoping that when the corpse was found it would expose the truth to the police.

Afterward for hours I walked the streets, but only those which were most poorly lighted. I remember passing the forever-burning garbage dump into which I hurled the wooden bar—but I said so already. I remember gradually figuring out that I'd been stupid. Weak and stupid. I should have finished him off and taken that gadget of his, which must also bear my prints, then found an expert who could bypass the booby traps it was no doubt infested with and recover the stored data . . .

But who? And where? And, anyhow, that might not prove a thing, except that someone somewhere had access to supertechnology and disguised it cleverly. Was that evidence for the ghastly scheme I had uncovered?

At last I did go back—and he had vanished. The Clerks of Domesday must have tracked him down.

Sooner or later they are bound to trace me

too. The state I was in when I handled that video camera, I must have left skin cells on it as well as prints, and probably by now their computers have already told them that they're looking for a man who dodged their fucking draft.

And does not accept, and to his dying day which may be all too close *will not* accept, the crazy tale that bastard fed me in that stinking alley. I'm to believe that in the future the world will devote two hundred years to inventing time machines, so as to send back phoney tourists to make notes and measurements of what is scheduled to be wrecked? What a load of balls! No, such rubbish has to be what I called it before: a hypnotic cover story. Faking their gear to look the way it did, they only made me believe the more that they were being paid by the sons-of-bitches who really truly plan to launch their countless bombs. And heaven only knows who they may be. They and all their kind are out of reach of you and me . . .

But their hireling clerks are still on duty, busy with their sick and loathsome task, all of them knowing that a date has been fixed for nuclear war, all of them no doubt assured of places in deep shelters, all with jobs to tackle afterwards in that sanitary Disneyland. And who cares about the real live human beings at Athens and Dubrovnik, Granada and Carcassonne?

Or the town you live in—you! Yes, *you!*

Look out for them! They may be on your street right now! They may be in a place you visit on vacation! You can tell them by the clues I've given. *Expose them at all costs!* Nail the lie their agent tried to sell me in that filthy alley, prevent the war, and—

Oh, Jesus.

There are four people coming this way through the dark, and they don't walk like ordinary strollers. They look wrong, just as the Japanese in Athens did. They move, they act, they practically smell, like traitors you could pay to make up lists of what we've been condemned to lose in World War III.

And why are they heading in my direction if they don't know who I am? And I'm too hungry and too weak to run.

Oh God, if you exist! Save me! If you can't save anybody else, save me because I reasoned out the truth!

But the trudging of those feet—*crush-crush, crush-crush*—sounds so much like the noise of distant bombs . . .

THURNLEY ABBEY

Perceval Landon

I thought long and hard about including this story, not because I had any doubts as to its merit—I find it pretty near as terrifying as it seemed to me when I first read it, most of thirty years ago—but because I thought it would be too familiar: Everett Bleiler's indispensable *Guide to Supernatural Fiction* (not to be confused with his excellent two-volume *Supernatural Fiction Writers*) lists six anthology appearances up to 1960. But so many of my readers have denied all knowledge of it that I'm delighted to introduce them to it here.

THREE YEARS AGO I was on my way out to the East, and as an extra day in London was of some importance I took the Friday evening mail-train to Brindisi instead of the usual Thursday morning Marseilles express. Many people shrink from the long forty-eight-hour train journey through Europe, and the subsequent rush across the Mediterranean on the nineteen-knot *Isis* or *Osiris*; but there is really very little discomfort on either the train or the mail-boat, and, unless there is actually nothing for me to do, I always like to save the extra day and a half in London before I say good-bye to her for one of my longer tramps.

This time—it was early, I remember, in the

shipping season, probably about the beginning of September—there were few passengers, and I had a compartment in the P. & O. Indian express to myself all the way from Calais. All Sunday I watched the blue waves dimpling the Adriatic, and the pale rosemary along the cuttings; the plain white towns, with their flat roofs and their bold *duomos*, and the grey-green, gnarled, olive orchards of Apulia. The journey was just like any other. We ate in the dining car as often and as long as we decently could. We slept after luncheon; we dawdled the afternoon away with yellow-backed novels; sometimes we exchanged platitudes in the smoking-room, and it was there that I met Alastair Colvin.

Colvin was a man of middle height, with a resolute, well-cut jaw; his hair was turning grey; his moustache was sun-whitened, otherwise he was clean shaven—obviously a gentleman, and obviously also a preoccupied man. He had no great wit. When spoken to, he made the usual remarks in the right way, and I dare say he refrained from banalities only because he spoke less than the rest of us; most of the time he buried himself in the Wagon-lit Company's time-table, but seemed unable to concentrate his attention on any one page of it. He found that I had been over the Siberian railway, and for a quarter of an hour he discussed it with me. Then he lost interest in it, and rose to go to his compartment. But he came back again very soon, and seemed glad to pick up the conversation again.

Of course this did not seem to me to be of any importance. Most travellers by train become a trifle infirm of purpose after thirty-six hours' rattling. But Colvin's restless way I noticed in somewhat marked contrast with the man's personal importance and dignity; especially ill-suited was it to his finely made, large hand with its strong, broad, regular nails and its few lines. As I looked at his hand I noticed a long, deep, and recent scar of ragged shape. However, it is absurd to pretend that I thought anything was unusual. I went off at five o'clock on Sunday afternoon to sleep away the hour or two that had still to be got through before we arrived at Brindisi.

Once there, we few passengers transshipped our hand baggage, verified our berths—there were only a score of us in all—and then, after an aimless ramble of half an hour in Brindisi, we returned to dinner at the Hotel International, not wholly surprised that the town had been the death of Virgil. If I remember rightly, there is a gaily painted hall at the International—I do not wish to advertise anything, but there is no other place in Brindisi at which to await the coming of the mails—and after dinner I was looking with awe at a trellis overgrown with blue vines, when

Colvin moved across the room to my table. He picked up *Il Secolo*, but almost immediately gave up the pretence of reading it. He turned squarely to me and said:

"Would you do me a favour?"

One doesn't do favours to stray acquaintances on Continental expresses without knowing something more of them than I knew of Colvin. But I smiled in a noncommittal way, and asked him what he wanted. I wasn't wrong in part of my estimate of him; he said bluntly:

"Will you let me sleep in your cabin on the *Osiris*?" And he coloured a little as he said it.

Now, there is nothing more tiresome than having to put up with a stable-companion at sea, and I asked him rather pointedly:

"Surely there is room for all of us?" I thought that perhaps he had been partnered off with some mangy Levantine, and wanted to escape from him at all hazards.

Colvin, still somewhat confused, said:

"Yes, I am in a cabin by myself. But you would do me the greatest favour if you would allow me to share yours."

This was all very well, but, besides the fact that I always sleep better when alone, there had been some recent thefts on board English liners, and I hesitated, frank and honest and self-conscious as Colvin was. Just then the mail-train came in with a clatter and a rush of escaping steam, and I asked him to see me again about it on the boat when we started. He answered me curtly—I suppose he saw the mistrust in my manner—"I am a member of White's." I smiled to myself as he said it, but I remembered in a moment that the man—if he were really what he claimed to be, and I make no doubt that he was—must have been sorely put to it before he urged the fact as a guarantee of his respectability to a total stranger at a Brindisi hotel.

That evening, as we cleared the red and green harbour lights of Brindisi, Colvin explained. This is his story in his own words.

"When I was travelling in India some years ago, I made the acquaintance of a youngish man in the Woods and Forests. We camped out together for a week, and I found him a pleasant companion. John Broughton was a lighthearted soul when off duty, but a steady and capable man in any of the small emergencies that continually arise in that department. He was liked and trusted by the natives, and, though a trifle overpleased with himself when he escaped to civilization at Simla or Calcutta, Broughton's future was well assured in Government service when a fair-sized estate was unexpectedly left to him, and he joyfully shook the dust of the Indian plains from his feet and returned to England.

"For five years he drifted about London. I saw

him now and then. We dined together about every eighteen months, and I could trace pretty exactly the gradual sickening of Broughton with a merely idle life. He then set out on a couple of long voyages, returned as restless as before, and at last told me that he had decided to marry and settle down at his place, Thurnley Abbey, which had long been empty. He spoke about looking after the property and standing for his constituency in the usual way. Vivien Wilde, his *fiancée*, had, I suppose, begun to take him in hand. She was a pretty girl with a deal of fair hair and rather an exclusive manner; deeply religious in a narrow school, she was still kindly and high-spirited, and I thought that Broughton was in luck. He was quite happy and full of information about his future.

"Among other things, I asked him about Thurnley Abbey. He confessed that he hardly knew the place. The last tenant, a man called Clarke, had lived in one wing for fifteen years and seen no one. He had been a miser and a hermit. It was the rarest thing for a light to be seen at the Abbey after dark. Only the barest necessities of life were ordered, and the tenant himself received them at the side door. His one half-caste manservant, after a month's stay in the house, had abruptly left without warning, and had returned to the Southern States.

"One thing Broughton complained bitterly

about: Clarke had wilfully spread the rumour among the villagers that the Abbey was haunted, and had even condescended to play childish tricks with spirit-lamps and salt in order to scare trespassers away at night. He had been detected in the act of this tomfoolery, but the story spread, and no one, said Broughton, would venture near the house, except in broad daylight. The hauntedness of Thurnley Abbey was now, he said with a grin, part of the gospel of the countryside, but he and his young wife were going to change all that. Would I propose myself any time I liked? I, of course, said I would, and equally, of course, intended to do nothing of the sort without a definite invitation.

"The house was put in thorough repair, though not a stick of the old furniture and tapestry was removed. Floors and ceilings were relaid; the roof was made watertight again, and the dust of half a century was scoured out. He showed me some photographs of the place. It was called an Abbey, though as a matter of fact it had been only the infirmary of the long-vanished Abbey of Closter some five miles away. The larger part of this building remained as it had been in pre-Reformation days, but a wing had been added in Jacobean times, and that part of the house had been kept in something like repair by Mr. Clarke. He had in both the ground and first floors set a heavy timber door, strongly barred with iron, in the passage between the earlier and the Jacobean parts of the house, and had entirely neglected the former. So there had been a good deal of work to be done.

"Broughton, whom I saw in London two or three times about this period, made a deal of fun over the positive refusal of the workmen to remain after sundown. Even after the electric light had been put into every room, nothing would induce them to remain, though, as Broughton observed, electric light was death on ghosts. The legend of the Abbey's ghosts had gone far and wide, and the men would take no risks. They went home in batches of five and six, and even during the daylight hours there was an inordinate amount of talking between one and another, if either happened to be out of sight of his companion. On the whole, though nothing of any sort or kind had been conjured up even by their heated imaginations during their five months' work upon the Abbey, the belief in the ghosts was rather strengthened than otherwise in Thurnley because of the men's confessed nervousness, and local tradition declared itself in favour of the ghost of an immured nun.

" 'Good old nun!' said Broughton.

"I asked him whether in general he believed in the possibility of ghosts, and, rather to my surprise, he said that he couldn't say he entirely disbelieved in them. A man in India had told him one morning in camp that he believed that his mother was dead in England, as her vision had come to his tent the night before. He had not been alarmed, but had said nothing, and the figure vanished again. As a matter of fact, the next possible *dak-walla* brought on a telegram announcing the mother's death. 'There the thing was,' said Broughton. But at Thurnley he was practical enough. He roundly cursed the idiotic selfishness of Clarke, whose silly antics had caused all the inconvenience. At the same time, he couldn't refuse to sympathize to some extent with the ignorant workmen. 'My own idea,' said he, 'is that if a ghost ever does come in one's way, one ought to speak to it.'

"I agreed. Little as I knew of the ghost world and its conventions, I had always remembered that a spook was in honour bound to wait to be spoken to. It didn't seem much to do, and I felt that the sound of one's own voice would at any rate reassure oneself as to one's wakefulness. But there are few ghosts outside Europe—few, that is, that a white man can see—and I had never been troubled with any. However, as I have said, I told Broughton that I agreed.

"So the wedding took place, and I went to it in a tall hat which I bought for the occasion, and the new Mrs. Broughton smiled very nicely at me afterwards. As it had to happen, I took the Orient Express that evening and was not in

England again for nearly six months. Just before I came back I got a letter from Broughton. He asked if I could see him in London or come to Thurnley, as he thought I should be better able to help him than anyone else he knew. His wife sent a nice message to me at the end, so I was reassured about at least one thing. I wrote from Budapest that I would come and see him at Thurnley two days after my arrival in London, and as I sauntered out of the Pannonia into the Kerepesi Utcza to post my letters, I wondered of what earthly service I could be to Broughton. I had been out with him after tiger on foot, and I could imagine few men better able at a pinch to manage their own business. However, I had nothing to do, so after dealing with some small accumulations of business during my absence, I packed a kit bag and departed to Euston.

"I was met by Broughton's great limousine at Thurnley Road station, and after a drive of nearly seven miles we echoed through the sleepy streets of Thurnley village, into which the main gates of the park thrust themselves, splendid with pillars and spread-eagles and tomcats rampant atop of them. I never was a herald, but I know that the Broughtons have the right to supporters—heaven knows why! From the gates a quadruple avenue of beech trees led inwards for a quarter of a mile. Beneath them a neat strip of fine turf edged the road and ran back until the poison of the dead beech leaves killed it under the trees. There were many wheel tracks on the road, and a comfortable little pony trap jogged past me laden with a country parson and his wife and daughter. Evidently there was some garden party going on at the Abbey. The road dropped away to the right at the end of the avenue, and I could see the Abbey across a wide pasturage and a broad lawn thickly dotted with guests.

"The end of the building was plain. It must have been almost mercilessly austere when it was first built, but time had crumbled the edges and toned the stone down to an orange-lichened grey wherever it showed behind its curtain of magnolia, jasmine, and ivy. Farther on was the three-storied Jacobean house, tall and handsome. There had not been the slightest attempt to adapt the one to the other, but the kindly ivy had glossed over the touching point. There was a tall *flèche* in the middle of the building, surmounting a small bell tower. Behind the house there rose the mountainous verdure of Spanish chestnuts all the way up the hill.

"Broughton had seen me coming from afar, and walked across from his other guests to welcome me before turning me over to the butler's care. This man was sandy-haired and rather inclined to be talkative. He could, however, answer hardly any questions about the house;

he had, he said, been there only three weeks. Mindful of what Broughton had told me, I made no inquiries about ghosts, though the room into which I was shown might have justified anything. It was a very large, low room with oak beams projecting from the white ceiling. Every inch of the walls, including the doors, was covered with tapestry, and a remarkably fine Italian four-post bedstead, heavily draped, added to the darkness and dignity of the place. All the furniture was old, well made, and dark. Underfoot there was a plain green pile carpet, the only new thing about the room except the electric light fittings and the jugs and basins. Even the looking-glass on the dressing table was an old pyramidal Venetian glass set in a heavy repoussé frame of tarnished silver.

"After a few minutes' cleaning up, I went downstairs and out upon the lawn, where I greeted my hostess. The people gathered there were of the usual country type, all anxious to be pleased and roundly curious as to the new master of the Abbey. Rather to my surprise, and quite to my pleasure, I rediscovered Glenham, whom I had known well in old days in Barotse-land; he lived quite close, as, he remarked with a grin, I ought to have known. 'But,' he added, 'I don't live in a place like this.' He swept his hand to the long, low lines of the Abbey in obvious admiration, and then, to my intense interest, muttered beneath his breath: 'Thank God!' He saw that I had overheard him, and turning to me said decidedly: 'Yes, "thank God" I said, and I meant it. I wouldn't live at the Abbey for all Broughton's money.'

" 'But surely,' I demurred, 'you know that old Clarke was discovered in the very act of setting light to his bug-a-boos?'

"Glenham shrugged his shoulders. 'Yes, I know about that. But there is something wrong with the place still. All I can say is that Broughton is a different man since he has lived here. I don't believe that he will remain much longer. But—you're staying here?—well, you'll hear all about it tonight. There's a big dinner, I understand.' The conversation turned off to old reminiscences, and Glenham soon after had to go.

"Before I went to dress that evening I had twenty minutes' talk with Broughton in his library. There was no doubt that the man was altered, gravely altered. He was nervous and fidgety, and I found him looking at me only when my eye was off him. I naturally asked him what he wanted of me. I told him I would do anything I could, but that I couldn't conceive what he lacked that I could provide. He said with a lustreless smile that there was, however, something, and that he would tell me the following morning. It struck me that he was somehow ashamed of himself, and perhaps ashamed of the part he was asking me to play. However, I dismissed the subject from my mind and went up to dress in my palatial room. As I shut the door a draught blew out the Queen of Sheba from the wall, and I noticed that the tapestries were not fastened to the wall at the bottom. I have always held very practical views about spooks, and it has often seemed to me that the slow waving in firelight of loose tapestry upon a wall would account for ninety-nine percent of the stories one hears. Certainly the dignified undulation of this lady with her attendants and huntsmen—one of whom was untidily cutting the throat of a fallow deer upon the very steps on which King Solomon, a grey-faced Flemish nobleman with the order of the Golden Fleece, awaited his fair visitor—gave colour to my hypothesis.

"Nothing much happened at dinner. The people were very much like those of the garden party. A young woman next me seemed anxious to know what was being read in London. As she was far more familiar than I with the most recent magazines and literary supplements, I found salvation in being myself instructed in the tendencies of modern fiction. All true art, she said, was shot through and through with melancholy. How vulgar were the attempts at wit that marked so many modern books! From the beginning of literature it had always been tragedy that embodied the highest attainment of every age. To call such works morbid merely begged the question. No thoughtful man—she looked sternly at me through the steel rim of her glasses—could fail to agree with her.

"Of course, as one would, I immediately and properly said that I slept with Pett Ridge and Jacobs under my pillow at night, and that if *Jorrocks* weren't quite so large and cornery, I would add him to the company. She hadn't read any of them, so I was saved—for a time. But I remember grimly that she said that the dearest wish of her life was to be in some awful and soul-freezing situation of horror, and I remember that she dealt hardly with the hero of Nat Paynter's vampire story, between nibbles at her brown-bread ice. She was a cheerless soul, and I couldn't help thinking that if there were many such in the neighbourhood it was not surprising that old Glenham had been stuffed with some nonsense or other about the Abbey. Yet nothing could well have been less creepy than the glitter of silver and glass, and the subdued lights and cackle of conversation all round the dinner table.

"After the ladies had gone I found myself talking to the rural dean. He was a thin, earnest man, who at once turned the conversation to old Clarke's buffooneries. But, he said, Mr.

Broughton had introduced such a new and cheerful spirit, not only into the Abbey but, he might say, into the whole neighbourhood, that he had great hopes that the ignorant superstitions of the past were from henceforth destined to oblivion. Thereupon his other neighbour, a portly gentleman of independent means and position, audibly remarked 'Amen', which damped the rural dean, and we talked of partridges past, partridges present, and pheasants to come. At the other end of the table Broughton sat with a couple of his friends, red-faced hunting men. Once I noticed that they were discussing me, but I paid no attention to it at the time. I remembered it a few hours later.

"By eleven all the guests were gone, and Broughton, his wife, and I were alone together under the fine plaster ceiling of the Jacobean drawing room. Mrs. Broughton talked about one or two of the neighbours, and then, with a smile, said that she knew I would excuse her, shook hands with me, and went off to bed. I am not very good at analysing things, but I felt that she talked a little uncomfortably and with a suspicion of effort, smiled rather conventionally, and was obviously glad to go. These things seem trifling enough to repeat, but I had throughout the faint feeling that everything was not square. Under the circumstances, this was enough to set me wondering what on earth the service could be that I was to render—wondering also whether the whole business were not some ill-advised jest in order to make me come down from London for a mere shooting party.

"Broughton said little after she had gone. But he was evidently labouring to bring the conversation round to the so-called haunting of the Abbey. As soon as I saw this, of course, I asked him directly about it. He then seemed at once to lose interest in the matter. There was no doubt about it: Broughton was somehow a changed man, and to my mind he had changed in no way for the better. Mrs. Broughton seemed no sufficient cause. He was clearly very fond of her, and she of him. I reminded him that he was going to tell me what I could do for him in the morning, pleaded my journey, lighted a candle, and went upstairs with him. At the end of the passage leading into the old house he grinned weakly and said: 'Mind, if you see a ghost, do talk to it; you said you would.' He stood irresolutely a moment and then turned away. At the door of his dressing room he paused once more: 'I'm here,' he called out, 'if you should want anything. Good night,' and he shut his door.

"I went along the passage to my room, undressed, switched on a lamp beside my bed, read a few pages of the *Jungle Book*, and then, more

than ready for sleep, turned the light off and
went fast asleep.

"Three hours later I woke up. There was not a
breath of wind outside. There was not even a
flicker of light from the fireplace. As I lay there,
an ash tinkled slightly as it cooled, but there was
hardly a gleam of the dullest red in the grate. An
owl cried among the silent Spanish chestnuts on
the slope outside. I idly reviewed the events of
the day, hoping that I should fall off to sleep
again before I reached dinner. But at the end I
seemed as wakeful as ever. There was no help
for it. I must read my *Jungle Book* again till I felt
ready to go off, so I fumbled for the pear at the
end of the cord that hung down inside the bed,
and I switched on the bedside lamp. The sudden
glory dazzled me for a moment. I felt under my
pillow for my book with half-shut eyes. Then,
growing used to the light, I happened to look
down to the foot of my bed.

"I can never tell you really what happened
then. Nothing I could ever confess in the most
abject words could even faintly picture to you
what I felt. I know that my heart stopped dead,
and my throat shut automatically. In one instinc-
tive movement I crouched back up against the
headboards of the bed, staring at the horror. The
movement set my heart going again, and the
sweat dripped from every pore. I am not a

particularly religious man, but I had always believed that God would never allow any supernatural appearance to present itself to man in such a guise and in such circumstances that harm, either bodily or mental, could result to him. I can only tell you that at that moment both my life and my reason rocked unsteadily on their seats."

The other *Osiris* passengers had gone to bed. Only he and I remained leaning over the starboard railing, which rattled uneasily now and then under the fierce vibration of the over-engined mail-boat. Far over, there were the lights of a few fishing smacks riding out the night, and a great rush of white combing and seething water fell out and away from us overside.

At last Colvin went on:

"Leaning over the foot of my bed, looking at me, was a figure swathed in a rotten and tattered veiling. This shroud passed over the head, but left both eyes and the right side of the face bare. It then followed the line of the arm down to where the hand grasped the bed-end. The face was not entirely that of a skull, though the eyes and the flesh of the face were totally gone. There was a thin, dry skin drawn tightly over the features, and there was some skin left on the hand. One wisp of hair crossed the forehead. It was perfectly still. I looked at it, and it looked at me, and my brains turned dry and hot in my head. I had still got the pear of the electric lamp in my hand, and I played idly with it; only I dared not turn the light out again. I shut my eyes only to open them in a hideous terror the same second. The thing had not moved. My heart was thumping, and the sweat cooled me as it evaporated. Another cinder tinkled in the gate, and a panel creaked in the wall.

"My reason failed me. For twenty minutes, or twenty seconds, I was able to think of nothing else but this awful figure, till there came, hurtling through the empty channels of my senses, the remembrance that Broughton and his friends had discussed me furtively at dinner. The dim possibility of its being a hoax stole gratefully into my unhappy mind, and once there, one's pluck came creeping back along a thousand tiny veins. My first sensation was one of blind, unreasoning thankfulness that my brain was going to stand the trial. I am not a timid man, but the best of us needs some human handle to steady him in time of extremity, and in this faint but growing hope that after all it might be only a brutal hoax, I found the fulcrum that I needed. At last I moved.

"How I managed to do it I cannot tell you, but with one spring towards the foot of the bed I got within arm's length and struck out one fearful blow with my fist at the thing. It crumbled under it, and my hand was cut to the bone. With a sickening revulsion after my terror, I dropped half-fainting across the end of the bed. So it was merely a foul trick after all. No doubt the trick had been played many a time before: no doubt Broughton and his friends had had some large bet among themselves as to what I should do when I discovered the gruesome thing. From my state of abject terror I found myself transported into an insensate anger. I shouted curses upon Broughton. I dived rather than climbed over the bed-end on to the sofa. I tore at the robed skeleton—how well the whole thing had been carried out, I thought—I broke the skull against the floor, and stamped upon its dry bones. I flung the head away under the bed, and rent the brittle bones of the trunk in pieces. I snapped the thin thighbones across my knee, and flung them in different directions. The shinbones I set up against a stool and broke with my heel. I raged like a Berserker against the loathly thing, and stripped the ribs from the backbone and slung the breastbone against the cupboard. My fury increased as the work of destruction went on. I tore the frail, rotten veil into twenty pieces, and the dust went up over everything, over the clean blotting paper and the silver inkstand.

"At last my work was done. There was but a

raffle of broken bones and strips of parchment and crumbling wool. Then, picking up a piece of the skull—it was the cheek and temple bone of the right side, I remember—I opened the door and went down the passage to Broughton's dressing room. I remember still how my sweat-dripping pyjamas clung to me as I walked. At the door I kicked and entered.

"Broughton was in bed. He had already turned the light on and seemed shrunken and horrified. For a moment he could hardly pull himself together. Then I spoke. I don't know what I said. I only know that from a heart full and overfull with hatred and contempt, spurred on by shame of my own recent cowardice, I let my tongue run on. He answered nothing. I was amazed at my own fluency. My hair still clung lankily to my wet temples, my hand was bleeding profusely, and I must have looked a strange sight. Broughton huddled himself up at the head of the bed just as I had. Still he made no answer, no defence. He seemed preoccupied with something beside my reproaches, and once or twice moistened his lips with his tongue. But he could say nothing, though he moved his hands now and then, just as a baby who cannot speak moves its hands.

"At last the door into Mrs. Broughton's room opened and she came in, white and terrified. 'What is it? What is it? Oh, in God's name, what is it?' she cried again and again, and then she went up to her husband and sat on the bed in her nightdress, and the two faced me. I told her what the matter was. I spared her husband not a word for her presence there. Yet he seemed hardly to understand. I told the pair that I had spoiled their cowardly joke for them. Broughton looked up.

"'I have smashed the foul thing into a hundred pieces,' I said. Broughton licked his lips again and his mouth worked. 'By God!' I shouted, 'it would serve you right if I thrashed you within an inch of your life. I will take care that no decent man or woman of my acquaintance ever speaks to you again. And there,' I added, throwing the broken piece of the skull upon the floor beside his bed—'there is a souvenir for you of your damned work tonight!'

"Broughton saw the bone, and in a moment it was his turn to frighten me. He squealed like a hare caught in a trap. He screamed and screamed till Mrs. Broughton, almost as bewildered as myself, held on to him and coaxed him like a child to be quiet. But Broughton—and as he moved I thought that ten minutes ago I perhaps looked as terribly ill as he did—thrust her from him, and scrambled out of the bed on to the floor, and still screaming put out his hand to the bone. It had blood on it from my hand. He paid no attention to me whatever. In truth I said

181

nothing. This was a new turn indeed to the horrors of the evening. He rose from the floor with the bone in his hand and stood silent. He seemed to be listening. 'Time, time, perhaps,' he muttered, and almost at the same moment fell at full-length on the carpet, cutting his head against the fender. The bone flew from his hand and came to rest near the door. I picked Broughton up, haggard and broken, with blood over his face. He whispered hoarsely and quickly: 'Listen, listen!' We listened.

"After ten seconds' utter quiet, I seemed to hear something. I could not be sure, but at last there was no doubt. There was a quiet sound as of one moving along the passage. Little regular steps came towards us over the hard oak flooring. Broughton moved to where his wife sat, white and speechless, on the bed, and pressed her face into his shoulder.

"Then, the last thing that I could see as he turned the light out, he fell forward with his own head pressed into the pillow of the bed. Something in their company, something in their cowardice, helped me, and I faced the open doorway of the room which was outlined fairly clearly against the dimly lighted passage. I put out one hand and touched Mrs. Broughton's shoulder in the darkness. But at the last moment I too failed. I sank on my knees and put my face in the bed. Only we all heard. The footsteps came to the door, and there they stopped. The piece of bone was lying a yard inside the door. There was a rustle of moving stuff, and the thing was in the room. Mrs. Broughton was silent; I could hear Broughton's voice praying, muffled in the pillow; I was cursing my own cowardice. Then the steps moved out again on the oak boards of the passage, and I heard the sounds dying away. In a flash of remorse I went to the door and looked out. At the end of the corridor I thought I saw something that moved away. A moment later the passage was empty. I stood with my forehead against the jamb of the door, almost physically sick.

" 'You can turn the light on,' I said, and there was an answering flare. There was no bone at my feet. Mrs. Broughton had fainted. Broughton was almost useless, and it took me ten minutes to bring her to. Broughton only said one thing worth remembering. For the most part he went on muttering prayers. But I was glad afterwards to recollect that he had said that thing. He said in a colourless voice, half as a question, half as a reproach: 'You didn't speak to her.'

"We spent the remainder of the night together. Mrs. Broughton actually fell off into a kind of sleep before dawn, but she suffered so horribly in her dreams that I shook her into consciousness again. Never was dawn so long in coming. Three or four times Broughton spoke to himself.

Mrs. Broughton would then just tighten her hold on his arm, but she could say nothing. As for me, I can honestly say that I grew worse as the hours passed and the light strengthened. The two violent reactions had battered down my steadiness of view, and I felt that the foundations of my life had been built upon the sand. I said nothing, and after binding up my hand with a towel I did not move. It was better so. They helped me and I helped them, and we all three knew that our reason had gone very near to ruin that night.

"At last, when the light came in pretty strongly, and the birds outside were chattering and singing, we felt that we must do something. Yet we never moved. You might have thought that we should particularly dislike being found as we were by the servants: yet nothing of that kind mattered a straw, and an overpowering listlessness found us as we sat, until Chapman, Broughton's man, actually knocked and opened the door. None of us moved. Broughton, speaking hardly and stiffly, said: 'Chapman, you can come back in five minutes.' Chapman was a discreet man, but it would have made no difference to us if he had carried his news to the 'room' at once.

"We looked at one another and I said I must go back. I meant to wait outside until Chapman returned. I simply dared not reenter my bedroom alone. Broughton roused himself and said that he would come with me. Mrs. Broughton agreed to remain in her own room for five minutes if the blinds were drawn up and all the doors left open.

"So Broughton and I, leaning stiffly one against the other, went down to my room. By the morning light that filtered past the blinds we could see our way, and I released the blinds. There was nothing wrong in the room from end to end, except smears of my own blood on the end of the bed, on the sofa, and on the carpet where I had torn the thing to pieces."

Colvin had finished his story. There was nothing to say. Seven bells stuttered out from the fo'c'sle, and the answering cry wailed through the darkness. I took him downstairs.

"Of course I am much better now, but it is a kindness of you to let me sleep in your cabin."

CUTTING DOWN
Bob Shaw

Bob Shaw has excelled at science fiction of all kinds, from the visionary (*The Palace of Eternity*) to the comic (*Who Goes Here*, full of the kind of humor that won him a Hugo Award), from the hard but human science fiction of *Orbitsville* to the fantastic world of *The Ragged Astronauts*. As you will see here and in my anthology *New Terrors*, he excels at horror too.

HERLEY WAS AWAKENED by the sounds of his wife getting out of bed. Afraid of seeing her nude body, he kept his eyes closed and listened intently as she padded about the room. There came a silky electrostatic crackling as she removed her nightdress—at which point he squeezed his eyes even more tightly shut—then a rustling of heavier material which told him she had donned a dressing gown. He relaxed and allowed the morning sun to penetrate his lashes with bright oily needles of light.

"What would you like for breakfast?" June Herley said.

He still avoided looking at her. "I'll have the usual—coffee and a cigarette." *That isn't*

189

enough, he added mentally. *Breakfast is the most important meal of the day.*

She paused at the bedroom door. "That isn't enough. Breakfast is the most important meal of the day."

"All right then—coffee and *two* cigarettes."

"Oh, *you!*" She went out on to the landing and he heard her wallowing progress all the way down the stairs and into the kitchen. Herley did not get up immediately. He cupped his hands behind his head and once again tried to fathom the mystery of what had happened to the girl he had married. It had taken a mere eight years for her to change from a slim vivacious creature into a hopeless, sagging hulk. In that time the flat cones of her breasts had become vast sloping udders, and the formerly boyish buttocks and thighs had turned into puckered sacks of fat which at the slightest knock developed multi-hued bruises which could persist for weeks. For the most part her face was that of a stranger, but there were times when he could discern the features of that other June, the one he had loved, impassively drowning beneath billows of pale tissue.

It was, he sometimes thought, the mental changes which frightened, sickened, baffled and enraged him the most. The other June would have endured any privation to escape from the tallowy prison of flesh, but the woman with whom he now shared his home blandly accepted her condition, aiding and abetting the tyrant of her stomach. Her latest self-deception—which was why she had begun to fuss about breakfast —was a diet which consisted entirely of protein and fat, to be eaten in any quantity desired as long as not the slightest amount of carbohydrate was consumed. Herley had no idea whether or not the system would work for other people, but he knew it had no chance in June's case. She used it as a justification for eating large greasy meals three or four times a day in his presence, and in between times—in his absence—filling up on sweet stuffs.

The aroma of frying ham filtering upwards from the kitchen was a reminder to Herley that his wife had yet to admit her new form of dishonesty. He got up and strode swiftly to the landing and down the stairs, moving silently in his bare feet, and opened the kitchen door. June was leaning over the opened pedal bin and eating chocolate ice cream from a plastic tub. On seeing him she gave a startled whimper and dropped the tub into the bin.

"It was almost empty," she said. "I was only . . ."

"It's all right—you're not committing any crime," he said, smiling. "My God, what sort of a life would it be if you couldn't enjoy your food?"

"I thought you . . ." June gazed at him, relieved but uncertain. "You must hate me for being like this."

"Nonsense!" Herley put his arms around his wife and drew her to him, appalled as always by the *looseness* of her flesh, the feeling that she was wrapped in a grotesque and ill-fitting garment. In his mid-thirties, he was tall and lean, with a bone structure and sparse musculature which could be seen with da Vincian clarity beneath taut dry skin. Watching the gradual invasion of June's body by adipose tissue had filled him with such a dread of a similar fate that he lived on a strictly fat-free diet and often took only one meal a day. In addition he exercised strenuously at least three times a week, determined to burn off every single oily molecule that might have insinuated itself into his system.

"I'll have my coffee as soon as it's ready," he said when he judged he had endured the bodily contact long enough. "I have to leave in thirty minutes."

"But this is your day off."

"Special story. I've got an interview lined up with Hamish Corcoran."

"Why couldn't it have been on a working day?"

"I was lucky to get him at all—he's practically a recluse since he quit the hospital."

"I know, poor man," June said reflectively. "They say the shock of what happened to his wife drove him out of his mind."

"They say lots of things that aren't worth listening to." Herley had no interest in the biochemist's personal life, only in a fascinating aspect of his work he had heard about for the first time a few nights earlier.

"Don't be so callous," June scolded. "I suppose if you came home and found that some psycho had butchered me you'd just shrug it off and go out looking for another woman."

"Not till after the funeral." Herley laughed aloud at his wife's expression. "Don't be silly, dear—you know I'd never put anybody in your place. Marriage is a once and for all time thing with me."

"I should hope so."

Herley completed his morning toilet, taking pleasure in stropping his open-bladed razor and shaving his flat-planed face to a shiny pinkness. He had a cup of black coffee for breakfast and left June still seated in the kitchen, the slabs of her hips overflowing her chair. She was lingering at the table with obvious intent, in spite of already having consumed enough calories to last the day. *There's no point in getting angry about it*, Herley thought. *Especially not today . . .*

He walked the mile to Aldersley station at a brisk pace, determined not to miss the early train to London. Hamish Corcoran had lived in Aldersley during his term at the hospital, but on retiring he had moved to a village near Reading, some sixty miles away on the far side of London, and reaching him was going to take a substantial part of the day. The journey was likely to be tiresome, but Herley had a feeling it was going to be worth his while. As a subeditor on the *Aldersley Post* he liked to supplement his income by turning in an occasional feature article written in his own time. Normally he would not have considered travelling more than a few miles on research—his leisure hours were too precious—but this was not a normal occasion, and the rewards promised to be greater than money.

As he had feared, the train and bus connections were bad, and it was nearly midday by the time he located the avenue of mature beeches and sun-splashed lawns in which Corcoran lived. Corcoran's was a classical turn-of-the-century, double-fronted house which was all but hidden from the road by banks of shrubbery. Herley felt a twinge of envy as he walked up the gravel drive—it appeared that becoming too eccentric to continue in employment, as Corcoran was reputed to have done, had not seriously affected his standard of living.

He rang the bell and waited, half-expecting the door to be opened by a housekeeper, but the grey-haired man who appeared was undoubtedly the owner. Hamish Corcoran was about sixty, round-shouldered and slight of build, with a narrow face in which gleamed humorous blue eyes and very white dentures. In spite of the summertime warmth he was wearing a heavy cardigan and a small woollen scarf, beneath which could be seen a starched collar and a blue bow tie.

"Hello, Mr. Corcoran," Herley said. "I phoned you yesterday. I'm Brian Herley, from the *Post*."

Corcoran gave him a fluorescent smile. "Come in, my boy, come in! It's very flattering that your editor should want to publish something about my work."

Herley decided against mentioning that nobody in the editorial office knew of his visit. "Well, the *Post* has always been interested in the research work at Aldersley, and we think the public should know more about its achievements."

"Quite right! Now, if you're anything like all the other gentlemen of the press I've met, you're not averse to a drop of malt. Is that right?"

"It *is* a rather thirsty sort of a day." Herley followed the older man into a cool brown room at the rear of the house and was installed in a leather armchair. He examined the room, while Corcoran was pouring drinks at a sideboard, and saw that the shelves which lined the walls were occupied by a jumble of books, official-looking reports and odd items of electronic equipment whose function was not apparent. Corcoran handed him a generous measure of whisky in a heavy crystal tumbler and sat down at the other side of a carved desk.

"And how are things in Aldersley?" Corcoran said, sipping his drink.

"Oh, much the same as ever."

"In other words, not worth talking about—especially after you've come such a long way to interview me." Corcoran took another sip of whisky and it dawned on Herley that the little man was quite drunk.

"I've got lots of time, Mr. Corcoran. Perhaps you could give me a general rundown, in layman's terms, on this whole business of slow muscles and fast muscles. I must confess I've never really understood what it was all about."

Corcoran looked gratified and immediately plunged into a moderately technical discourse on his work on nerve chemistry, speaking with the eager fluency of one who has for a long time been deprived of an audience. Herley pretended to be interested, even making written notes from time to time, waiting for the opportunity to discuss the real reason for his visit. He already knew that the research unit at Aldersley General had been involved in discoveries concerning the basic structure of muscle tissue. Experiments had shown that "fast" muscles such as those of the leg could be changed into "slow" muscles—like those of the abdomen—simply by severing the main nerves and reconnecting them to the wrong set, in a process analogous to reversing the leads from a battery.

The implication had been that type of muscle was determined, not by a genetic blueprint, but by some factor in the incoming nerve impulses. Hamish Corcoran had come up with a theory that the phenomenon was caused by a trophic chemical which trickled from nerve to muscle. He had already begun work on identifying and isolating the chemical involved when the tragedy of his wife's death had interrupted his researches. Soon afterwards he had been persuaded to retire. The rumor which had circulated in Aldersley was that he had gone mad, but no details had ever become public, thanks to a vigorous covering up job by a hospital which had no wish to see its reputation endangered.

"I was quite wrong about the chemical nature of the nerve influence," Corcoran was saying. "It has since been established that electrical stimulus is the big factor—slow muscles receive a fairly continuous low-frequency signal, fast muscles receive brief bursts at a much higher frequency—but the fascinating thing about the science game is the way in which one's mistakes can be so valuable. You can set off for China, so to speak, and discover America. In my case, America was a drug which offered complete and effortless control of obesity."

The final statement alerted Herley like a plunge into cold water.

"That's rather interesting," he said. "Control

of obesity, eh? I would have thought there was a huge commercial potential there."

"You would have thought wrong, my boy."

"Oh? Do you mean it wasn't possible to manufacture the drug?"

"Nothing of the sort! I was able to produce a pilot batch with very little difficulty." Corcoran glanced towards a bookshelf on his right, then noticed that his glass was empty. He stood up and went to the sideboard, for the third time during the interview, to pour himself a fresh drink. Herley took the opportunity to scan the shelf which had drawn the older man's gaze and his attention was caught by a small red box. It was heavily ornamented and cheap looking, the sort of thing that was turned out in quantity for the foreign souvenir market, and seemed more than a little out of place in its surroundings.

That's where the pills are, Herley thought, savagely triumphant. Until that moment he had suffered from lingering doubts about the information he had received from a drunken laboratory technician a few nights earlier. He had been talking to the technician in a bar, halfheartedly following up a lead about administrative malpractice in the hospital, when the tip on the story about Corcoran's secret wonder drug had surfaced through a sea of irrelevancies. It had cost Herley quite a bit of money to obtain what little information he had, and he also had been forced to acknowledge the possibility that—as sometimes happens to newsmen—he had been skilfully conned. Until the moment when Corcoran had glanced at the red box . . .

"Why aren't you drinking, young man?" Corcoran said with mock peevishness, returning to his desk. His voice was still crisp and clear, but triangles of crimson had appeared on his cheeks and his gait was noticeably unsteady.

Herley took a miniature sip of his original drink, barely wetting his lips. "One is enough for me on an empty stomach."

"Ah, yes." Corcoran ran his gaze over Herley's lean frame. "You don't eat much, do you?"

"Not a lot. I like to control my weight."

Corcoran nodded. "Very wise. Much better than letting your weight control you."

"There's no chance of that." Herley laughed comfortably.

"It's no laughing matter, my boy," Corcoran said. "I'm speaking quite literally—when the adipose tissue in a person's body achieves a certain threshold mass it can, *quite literally*, begin to govern that person's actions. It can take over that person's entire life."

For the first time in the interview Herley detected a trace of irrationality in his host's words, the first confirmation of the old rumors of eccentricity. Corcoran seemed to be talking fancifully, at the very least, and yet something in what he was saying was generating a strange disturbance in Herley's mind. How many times had he asked himself why it was that June, once so meticulous about her appearance, now allowed herself to be dominated by her appetite?

"Some people are a bit short on willpower," he said. "They get into the habit of overeating."

"Do you really believe that's all there is to it? Doesn't that strike you as being very strange?"

"Well, I . . ."

"Consider the case of a young woman who has become grossly overweight," Corcoran cut in, speaking very quickly and with an azure intensity in his eyes. "I choose the example of a woman because women traditionally place greater value on physical acceptability. Consider the case of a young woman who is say fifty percent or more above her proper weight. She is ugly, pathetic, *ill*. She is either socially ostracized or elects to cut herself off from social contact. Her chances of sexual fulfillment are almost zero, her life expectancy is greatly reduced, and the years she can anticipate promise nothing but sickness and self-disgust and unhappiness. Do you get the picture?"

"Yes." Herley moved uneasily in his chair.

"Now we come to the truly significant aspect of the case, and it is this. That woman *knows* that her suffering is unnecessary, that she can escape from her torment, that she can transform her physical appearance. She can become slim, healthy, attractive, energetic. She can avail herself of all that life has to offer. There's very little to it—all she has to do is eat a normal diet. It's a ridiculously trivial price to pay, the greatest bargain of all time—like being offered a million pounds for your cast-off socks—but what happens?" Corcoran paused to take a drink and the glass chattered momentarily against his teeth.

"Actually, I've seen what happens," Herley said, wondering where the discourse was leading. "She goes right on eating more than her body needs."

Corcoran shook his head. "That's the orthodox and simplistic view, my boy. She goes on eating more than she, as the original person, needs—but, in fact, she is eating exactly the right amount to suit the needs of the adipose organ."

Herley's uneasiness increased. "I'm sorry. I'm afraid I don't quite . . ."

"I'm talking about fat," Corcoran said fervently. "What do you know about fat?"

"Well . . . what is there to know about it? Isn't it just like lard?"

"A common misconception. Human body fat is actually a very complex substance which acts like a very large organ. Most people think of the adipose organ as having a poor blood supply, probably because it's pale and bleeds little during surgery, but in fact it has a very extensive blood supply in very small capillaries, and the density of those capillaries is greater than in muscle, second only to liver. More important, the adipose organ also has a subtle network of nerves which are locked into the central nervous system and capable of reacting with it."

Corcoran took another drink, eyeing Herley over the rim of his glass. "Do you understand what I'm saying?"

"No." Herley gave an uncertain laugh. "Not really."

Corcoran leaned forward, red pennants flaring on his cheeks. "I'm telling you that the adipose organ has a life of its own. It behaves like any other successful parasite—selfishly, looking out for its own interests. It controls its own environment as best it can, which means that it controls its host. That's why obese people have the compulsion to go on overeating, to go on being fat—no adipose organ willingly allows itself to be killed!"

Herley stared back at the older man with real anxiety in his heart. He had always had a phobia about insanity, and now he was experiencing a powerful urge to flee.

"That's a very . . . interesting theory," he said, draining his glass to banish the sudden dryness of his mouth.

"It's more than a theory," Corcoran replied. "And it explains why a person who tries to slim down finds it harder and harder to keep to a diet—when the adipose organ feels threatened it fights more strongly for its life. A person who loses *some* adipose tissue almost always puts it back on again. It's only in the very rare cases where the determined dieter manages to starve the adipose organ down below its threshold mass for autonomous consciousness that he successfully normalizes his weight. Then dieting suddenly becomes easy, and he tends to remain slim for life."

Herley did his best to appear unruffled. "This is really fascinating, but I don't see how it tallies with what you said earlier. Surely, if it were possible to produce a drug that would effectively . . . ah . . . kill this . . . ah . . . adipose organ, it would have tremendous commercial potential."

"The drug *can* be manufactured," Corcoran said, again glancing to his right. "I told you I had produced a pilot batch, in the form of a targeted liposome. For a human adult, four one-cubic-centimeter doses at daily intervals is enough to guarantee permanent normalization of body weight."

"Then what's the problem?"

"Why, the adipose organ itself," Corcoran said with an indulgent smile. "It fights very effectively against a slow death—so how do you imagine it would react to the prospect of a sudden death? Without understanding what was happening inside his own body and nervous system the patient would feel a powerful aversion to the use of the drug and would go to any lengths to avoid it. I think that takes care of your commercial potential."

This is getting crazier and crazier, Herley thought.

"What if you disguised the drug?" he said. "Or what if it was administered by force?"

"I don't think the adipose organ would be deceived, especially after the first dose—and there *is* such a thing as the medical ethic."

Herley stared into Corcoran's flushed countenance, wondering what to do next. It was easy to see why Aldersley General had decided to part company with Corcoran on the quiet. Although a brilliant pioneer in his field, the man was obviously deranged. Had it not been for the independent evidence from the laboratory technician, Herley would have had severe doubts about the efficacy of Corcoran's radical new drug. Now the substance seemed less attainable and therefore more desirable than ever.

"If that's the case," Herley said tentatively, "I don't suppose you'd ever be interested in selling the pilot batch?"

"*Sell* it!" Corcoran gave a wheezing laugh.

"Not for a million pounds, my boy. Not for a billion."

"I have to admire your principles, sir—I'm afraid I'd be tempted by a few hundred," Herley said with a rueful grimace, getting to his feet and dropping his notebook into his pocket. "It's been a pleasure talking to you, but I have to get back to Aldersley now."

"It's been more of a pleasure for me—I get very bored living in this big house all by myself since my . . ." Corcoran stood up and shook Herley's hand across his desk. "Don't forget to let me have a copy."

"A copy? Oh, yes. I'll send you half-a-dozen when the article is printed." Herley paused and looked beyond Corcoran towards the garden which lay outside the room's bay window. "That's a handsome shrub, isn't it? The one with the grey leaves."

Corcoran turned to look through the window. "Ah, yes. My *Olearia scilloniensis*. It does very well in this soil."

Herley, moving with panicky speed, side-stepped to the bookshelves on his left, snatched the red box from its resting place and slipped it inside his jacket, holding it between his arm and rib cage. He was back in his original position when Corcoran left the window and came to usher him out of the room. Corcoran steadied himself by touching his desk as he passed it.

"Thanks again," Herley said, trying to sound casual in spite of the hammering of his heart. "Don't bother coming to the front door with me—I can see myself out."

"I'm sure you can, but there's just one thing before you go."

Herley drew his lips into a stiff smile. "What's that, Mr. Corcoran?"

"I want my belongings back." Corcoran extended one hand. "The box you took from the shelf—I want it back. *Now!*"

"I don't know what you're talking about," Herley said, trying to sound both surprised and offended. "If you're suggesting . . ."

He broke off, genuinely surprised this time, as Corcoran lunged forward and tried to plunge his hands inside his jacket. Herley blocked the move, striving to push Corcoran away from him and being thwarted by the little man's unexpected strength and tenacity. The two men revolved in an absurd shuffling dance, then Herley's superior power manifested itself with an abrupt breaking of Corcoran's hold. Corcoran was forcibly propelled backwards for the distance of one pace and was jolted to a halt by the edge of the marble fireplace, which caught him at the base of skull. His eyes turned upwards on the instant, blind crescents of white, and blood spurted from his nose. He dropped into the hearth amid an appalling clatter of fire irons, and lay very, very still.

"You did that yourself," Herley accused, backing away, mumbling through the fingers he had pressed to his lips. "That's what you get for drinking too much. That's . . ."

He stopped speaking and, driven by a pounding sense of urgency, looked around the room for evidence of his visit. The whisky tumbler he had used was still sitting on the arm of the leather chair. He picked it up in trembling fingers, dried and polished it with his handkerchief and placed it among others on the sideboard, then went to the desk. Among the papers scattered on its surface he found a large business diary which was open at the current date. He examined the relevant page, making sure there was no note of his appointment, then hurried out of the room without looking at the obscene object in the hearth.

Herley felt an obscure and dull surprise on discovering that the world outside the house was exactly as he had left it—warm and green, placidly summery, unconcerned. Even the patterns of sunlight and leafy shadow looked the same, as though the terrible event in Corcoran's study had taken place in another continuum where time did not exist.

Grateful for the screening effect of the trees

and tall shrubs, Herley tightened his grip on the red box and started out for home.

"It's wonderful," June breathed, unable to divert her gaze from the small bottle which Herley had set on the kitchen table. "It seems too good to be true."

"But it *is* true—I guarantee it." Herley picked up the hypodermic syringe he had found in the red box and examined its tip. He had made important decisions on the journey back from Reading. His wife already knew where he had been during the day, so there was nothing to do but wait until the news of Corcoran's "accidental" death came out and then utter appropriate words. If the body was found quickly: *Good God! It must have happened to the poor man soon after I left him—but I don't think there's any point in my getting mixed up in an inquest, do you*? If, as was quite possible, there was a lengthy delay before the corpse came to light: *Fancy that! I wonder if it could have happened around the time I went to see him . . .*

In either case, to prevent June talking about it and perhaps forging links in other people's minds, he was going to lie about where and how he had obtained the drug.

"Just think, darling," he said enthusiastically. "Four little shots is all it will take. No dieting, no boring counting of calories, no trouble. I promise you, you're going to be your old self again."

June glanced down at her squablike breasts and the massive curvature of her stomach which the loosest fitting dress was unable to disguise. "It would be wonderful to wear nice clothes again."

"We'll get you a wardrobe full of them. Dresses, undies, swimsuits—the lot."

She gave a delighted laugh. "Do you really think I could go on the beach again?"

"You're *going*, dear—in a black bikini."

"Mmm! I can't wait."

"Neither can I." Herley opened the small bottle, inverted it and filled the hypodermic with colorless fluid. He had been disappointed to discover that the drug was not in tablet form, which he could have slipped unannounced into June's food, but there was nothing he could do to alter the situation. It was fortunate, he realized, that he knew how to use a needle.

"I don't think we need bother about sterilizing swabs and all that stuff," he said. "Give me your arm, dear."

June's eyes locked with his and her expression became oddly wary. "Now?"

"What do you mean now? Of course it's now. Give me your arm."

"But it's so soon. I need time to think."

"About what?" Herley demanded. "You don't think I'm planning to poison you, I hope."

"I . . . I don't even know where that stuff came from."

"It's from one of the best Harley Street clinics, June. It's something brand new, and it cost me a fortune."

June's lips had begun to look bloodless. "Well, why doesn't the doctor give me the injections himself?"

"For an extra hundred guineas? Talk sense!"

"I am talking sense—giving injections is a skilled job."

"You saw me giving dozens of them to your mother."

"Yes," June said heatedly. "And my mother died."

Herley gaped at her, unable to accept what he had heard. "June! Is that remark supposed to contain any kind of logic? It was *because* your mother was dying that she was on morphine."

"I don't care." June turned her back on him and walked towards the refrigerator, the great slabs of her hips working beneath the flowered material of her dress. "I'm not going to be rushed into anything."

Herley looked from her to the syringe in his hand and blood thundered in his ears. He hit her with the left side of his body, throwing her against the refrigerator and pinning her there while his left arm clamped around her neck. She heaved against him convulsively, once, then froze into immobility as the needle ran deep into the hanging flesh of her upper right arm. Herley was reminded of some wild creature which was genetically conditioned to yield at the moment of being taken by a predator, but the pang of guilt he felt served only to increase his anger. He drove a roughly estimated cubic centimeter of the fluid into his wife's bloodstream, withdrew the needle and stepped back, his breath coming in a series of low growls which he was unable to suppress.

June clamped her left hand over the bright red welt which had appeared on her arm, and turned to face him. "Did I deserve that, Brian?" she said sadly and gently. "Do I really deserve that sort of treatment?"

"Don't try your old Saint June act on me," he snapped. "It used to work, but things are going to be different from now on."

A fine rain began to fall in mid-evening, denying Herley the solace of working in the garden. He sat near the window in the front room, pretending to read a book and covertly watching June as she whiled away the hours before bed. She maintained a wounded silence, staring at the dried flower arrangement which screened the unused fireplace. At intervals of fifteen minutes she went foraging in the kitchen, and on her returns made no attempt to hide the fact that she was chewing. Once she brought back an economy-size container of salted peanuts and steadily munched her way through them, filling the whole room with the choking smell of peanut oil and saliva.

Herley endured the performance without comment, his mood a strange blend of boredom and terror. Slipping away from Corcoran's house could have been, he saw in retrospect, a serious blunder. It might have been better to telephone the police immediately and present them with a perfectly credible, unimpeachable story about Corcoran getting drunk and falling backwards against the mantelpiece. That way he could have kept the drug, hiding it in his pocket, and emerged from the affair free and clear. As it was, he was going to have some difficult explaining to do should the authorities manage to connect him with Corcoran's death.

Why couldn't the little swine have been reasonable? Herley repeated the question to himself many times during the dismal suburban evening and always arrived at the same answer. Anybody who was crazy enough to regard subcutaneous fat, simple disgusting blubber, as having sentience and a pseudolife of its own was hardly likely to listen to reason in any other respect. The very idea was enough to give Herley a cold, crawling sensation along his spine, adding a hint of Karloffian horror to the evening's natural gloom.

As the rain continued the air in the house steadily grew cooler and more humid, beginning to smell of toadstools, and Herley wished he had lit the fire hours earlier. He also found himself longing, uncharacteristically, for an alcoholic drink—regardless of the empty calories it would have represented—but there was nothing in the house. He contented himself by smoking cigarette after cigarette.

At 11:30 he stood up and said, "I think that's enough hilarity for one evening—are you going to bed?"

"Bed?" June looked up at him, seemingly without understanding. "Bed?"

"Yes, the thing we sleep on." *My God*, he thought, *what if I've given her the wrong drug? Maybe I jumped to the wrong conclusion about what Corcoran kept in the box.*

"I'll be up shortly," June said. "I'm just thinking about . . . everything."

"Look, I'm sorry about what happened earlier. I did it for *us*, you understand. It's a medical fact that overweight people develop an unreasoning fear of anything which threatens to . . ." Herley abruptly stopped speaking as he realized he had garnered his medical "fact" from some of Hamish Corcoran's wilder ramblings. He stared down at his wife, wondering if it could be only an effect of his disturbed mental state that she seemed more gross than ever, her head—in his foreshortened view—tiny in comparison to the settled alpine slopes of her body.

"Don't forget to lock up," he said, turning away to hide his repugnance.

When he got to bed a few minutes later the coolness of the sheets was relaxing and he realized with some surprise that he would have no trouble in falling asleep. He turned off his bedside lamp, plunging the room into almost total darkness, and allowed his thoughts to drift. The day had undoubtedly been the worst of his life, but if he kept his head there was absolutely nothing the police could pin on him. And as regards the trouble over the injections, June's attitude was bound to change by morning when she found there were no ill effects. Everything was going to be all right, after all . . .

Herley awoke very briefly a short time later when his wife came to bed. He listened to the sound of her undressing in the darkness, the familiar sighs and grunts punctuated by the crackle of static. When she lay down beside him he placed a companionable hand on her shoulder, taking the risk of the gesture being interpreted sexually, and within seconds was sinking down through layers of sleep, grateful for the surcease of thought.

The dream was immediately recognizable as such because in it his mother was still alive. Herley was two years old and his father was away on a business trip, so Herley was allowed to share his mother's bed. She was reading until the small hours of the morning and, as always when her husband was away, was eating from a dish of homemade fudge, occasionally handing a fragment to the infant Herley. She was a big woman, and as he lay close her back seemed as high as a wall—a warm, comforting, living wall which would protect him forever against all the uncertainties and threats of the outside world. Herley smiled and burrowed in closer, but something had begun to go wrong. The wall was shifting, bearing down on him. His mother was rolling over, engulfing him with her flesh, and it was impossible for him to cry out because the yielding substance of her was blocking his nose and mouth, and she was going to suffocate him without even realizing what was happening . . .

Mother!

Herley awoke to darkness and the terrifying discovery that he really was suffocating.

Something warm, heavy and slimy was pressing down over his face, and he could feel the moist weight of it on his chest. He clawed the object away from his mouth, but was only partially successful in dislodging it because it seemed to have an affinity for his skin, clinging with the tenacity of warm pitch. His fingers penetrated its surface and slid away again on a slurry of warm fluids.

Whimpering with panic, Herley heaved himself up off the pillow and groped for the switch of the bedside light. He turned it on. From the corner of one eye he glimpsed what had once been his wife lying beside him, her naked body bloody and strangely deflated, the skin burst into crimson tatters. The horror of the sight remained peripheral, however, because his own body was submerged in a pale, glistening mass of tissue, the surface of which was a network of fine blood vessels.

He screamed as he tried to tear the loathsome substance away. It ripped into quivering blubbery strips, but refused to be separated from him, clinging, sucking, tonguing him in dreadful intimacy.

Herley stopped screaming, entering a new realm of terror, as he discovered that the sluglike mass was somehow penetrating his skin, invading the sanctum of his body.

He got to his feet, dragging the glutinous burden with him, and in a lurching, caroming run reached the adjoining bathroom. Almost of their own accord, his fingers located and opened the bone-handled razor, and he began to cut.

Heedless of the fact that he was also inflicting

dreadful wounds on himself, he went on cutting and cutting and cutting . . .

Detective-Sergeant Bill Myers came out of the bathroom, paused on the landing to light a cigarette, and rejoined his senior officer in the front bedroom. "I've been in this business a hell of a long time," he said, "but those two are enough to make me spew. I've never seen anything like it."

"I have," Inspector Barraclough replied somberly, nodding at the lifeless figure on the bed. "This is the way we found Hamish Corcoran's wife a couple of years ago, but we managed to keep the details out of the papers—you know how it is with false confessions and copycat murders these days. It looks as though we'll be able to close the file on that case, thank God."

"You think this man Herley was a psycho?"

Barraclough nodded. "He's obviously been lying low for a couple of years, but we've established that he went to Corcoran's house yesterday. Killing Corcoran must have triggered him off somehow—so he came home and did this."

"It's his wife I feel sorry for." Myers moved closer to the bed and forced himself to examine what lay there, his eyes mirroring unprofessional sympathy. "Skinny little thing, wasn't she?"

THE
NECROMANCER

Arthur Gray

Sir Arthur Gray was a master of Jesus College in Cambridge. As "Ingulphus" he wrote *Tedious Brief Tales of Granta and Gramarye*, a collection of ghost stories in the antiquarian tradition of M. R. James, a book as rare and yellowed now as the books James's characters often had good reason to wish they had never opened. My search for his estate proved to be Jamesian in itself, especially when Sir Arthur's surviving relative was found to live in a place called Chillyhill Lane. Any of my readers who would like to read another brief, but hardly tedious, tale may find Gray's "The Everlasting Club" in Jack Sullivan's fine anthology *Lost Souls*.

THIS IS A story of Jesus College, and it relates to the year 1643. In that year Cambridge town was garrisoned for the Parliament by Colonel Cromwell and the troops of the Eastern Counties' Association. Soldiers were billeted in all the colleges, and contemporary records testify to their violent behaviour and the damage which they committed in the chambers which they occupied. In the previous year the Master of Jesus College, Doctor Sterne, was arrested by Cromwell when he was leaving the chapel, conveyed to London, and there imprisoned in the Tower. Before the summer of 1643 fourteen of the sixteen Fellows were expelled, and during the whole of that year there were, besides the soldiers, only some ten or twelve occupants of the college. The names of the two Fellows who were not ejected were John Boyleston and Thomas Allen.

With Mr. Boyleston this history is only concerned for the part which he took on the occasion of the visit to the college of the notorious fanatic, William Dowsing. Dowsing came to Cambridge in December, 1642, armed with powers to put in execution the ordinance of Parliament for the reformation of churches and chapels. Among the devastations committed by this ignorant clown, and faithfully recorded by him in his diary, it stands on record that on December 28, in the presence and perhaps with the approval of John Boyleston, he "digg'd up the steps (*i.e.* of the altar) and brake down Superstitions and Angels, 120 at the least." Dowsing's account of his proceedings is supplemented by the Latin History of the college, written in the reign of Charles II, by one of the Fellows, a certain Doctor John Sherman. Sherman records, but Dowsing does not, that there was a second witness of the desecration— Thomas Allen. Of the two he somewhat enigmatically remarks: "The one (*i.e.* Boyleston) stood behind a curtain to witness the evil work: the other, afflicted to behold the exequies of his

Alma Mater, made his life a filial offering at her grave, and, to escape the hands of wicked rebels, laid violent hands on himself."

That Thomas Allen committed suicide seems a fairly certain fact: and that remorse for the part which he had unwillingly taken in the sacrilege of December 28 prompted his act we may accept on the testimony of Sherman. But there is something more to tell which Sherman either did not know or did not think fit to record. His book deals only with the college and its society. He had no occasion to remember Adoniram Byfield.

Byfield was a chaplain attached to the Parliamentary forces in Cambridge, and quarters were assigned to him in Jesus College, in the first floor room above the gate of entrance. Below his chamber was the Porter's lodge, which at that time served as the armoury of the troopers who occupied the college. Above it, on the highest floor of the gate tower, "kept" Thomas Allen. These were the only rooms on the staircase. At the beginning of the Long Vacation of 1643 Allen was the only member of the college who continued to reside.

Some light is thrown on the character of Byfield and his connection with this story by a pudgy volume of old sermons of the Commonwealth period which is contained in the library of the college. Among the sermons which are bound up in it is one which bears the date 1643 and is designated on the title page:

A FAITHFUL ADMONICION of the Baalite sin of *Enchanters & Stargazers*, preacht to the Colonel Cromwell's Souldiers in Saint Pulcher's (*i.e.* Saint Sepulchre's) church, in Cambridge, by the fruitfull Minister, *Adoniram Byfield*, late departed unto God, in the yeare 1643, touching that of *Acts* the seventh, verse 43, *Ye took up the Tabernacle of Moloch, the Star of your god Remphan, figures which ye made to worship them; & I will carrie you away beyond Babylon.*

The discourse, in its title as in its contents, reveals its author as one of the fanatics who wrought on the ignorance and prejudice against "carnal" learning which actuated the Cromwellian soldiers in their brutal usage of the University "scholars" in 1643. All Byfield's learning was contained in one book—*the* Book. For him the revelation which gave it sufficed for its interpretation. What needed Greek to the man who spoke mysteries in unknown tongues, or the light of comment to him who was carried in the spirit into the radiance of the third heaven?

Now Allen, too, was an enthusiast, lost in

mystic speculation. His speculation was in the then novel science of mathematics and astronomy. Even to minds not darkened by the religious mania that possessed Byfield, that science was clouded with suspicion in the middle of the seventeenth century. Anglican, Puritan, and Catholic were agreed in regarding its great exponent, Descartes, as an atheist. Mathematicians were looked upon as necromancers, and Thomas Hobbes says that in his days at Oxford the study was considered to be "smutched with the black art," and fathers, from an apprehension of its malign influence, refrained from sending their sons to that University. How deep the prejudice had sunk into the soul of Adoniram his sermon shows. The occasion which suggested it was this. A pious cornet, leaving a prayer meeting at night, fell down one of the steep, unlighted staircases of the college and broke his neck. Two or three of the troopers were taken with a dangerous attack of dysentery. There was talk of these misadventures among the soldiers, who somehow connected them with Allen and his studies. The floating gossip gathered into a settled conviction in the mind of Adoniram.

For Allen was a mysterious person. Whether it was because he was engrossed in his studies, or that he shrank from exposing himself to the insults of the soldiers, he seldom showed himself outside his chamber. Perhaps he was tied to it by the melancholy to which Sherman ascribed his violent end. In his three months' sojourn on Allen's staircase Byfield had not seen him a dozen times, and the mystery of his closed door awakened the most fantastic speculations in the chaplain's mind. For hours together, in the room above, he could hear the mumbled tones of Allen's voice, rising and falling in ceaseless flow. No answer came, and no word that the listener could catch conveyed to his mind any intelligible sense. Once the voice was raised in a high key and Byfield distinctly heard the ominous ejaculation, "Avaunt, Sathanas, avaunt!" Once through his partly open door he had caught sight of him standing before a board chalked with figures and symbols which the imagination of Byfield interpreted as magical. At night, from the court below, he would watch the astrologer's lighted window, and when Allen turned his perspective glass upon the stars the conviction became rooted in his watcher's mind that he was living in perilous neighbourhood to one of the peeping and muttering wizards of whom the Holy Book spoke.

An unusual occurrence strengthened the suspicions of Byfield. One night he heard Allen creep softly down the staircase past his room; and, opening his door, he saw him disappear round the staircase foot, candle in hand. Silently, in the dark, Byfield followed him and saw him pass into the Porter's lodge. The soldiers were in bed and the armoury was unguarded. Through the lighted pane he saw Allen take down a horse pistol from a rack on the wall. He examined it closely, tried the lock, poised it as if to take aim, then replaced it and, leaving the lodge, disappeared up the staircase with his candle. A world of suspicions rushed on Byfield's mind, and they were not allayed when the soldiers reported in the morning that the pistols were intact. But one of the sick soldiers died that week.

Brooding on this incident Adoniram became more than ever convinced of the Satanic purposes and powers of his neighbour, and his suspicions were confirmed by another mysterious circumstance. As the weeks passed he became aware that at a late hour of night Allen's door was quietly opened. There followed a patter of scampering feet down the staircase, succeeded by silence. In an hour or two the sound came back. The patter went up the stairs to Allen's chamber, and then the door was closed. To lie awake waiting for this ghostly sound became a horror to Byfield's diseased imagination. In his bed he prayed and sang psalms to be relieved of it. Then he abandoned thoughts of sleep and would sit up waiting if he might surprise and detect this walking terror of the night. At first in the darkness of the stairs it eluded him. One night, light in hand, he managed to get a glimpse of it as it disappeared at the foot of the stairs. It was shaped like a large black cat.

Far from allaying his terrors, the discovery awakened new questionings in the heart of Byfield. Quietly he made his way up to Allen's door. It stood open and a candle burnt within. From where he stood he could see each corner of the room. There was the board scribbled with hieroglyphs; there were the magical books open on the table; there were the necromancer's instruments of unknown purpose. But there was no live thing in the room, and no sound save the rustling of papers disturbed by the night air from the open window.

A horrible certitude seized on the chaplain's mind. This Thing that he had caught sight of was no cat. It was the Evil One himself, or it was the wizard translated into animal shape. On what foul errand was he bent? Who was to be his new victim? With a flash there came upon his mind the story how Phinehas had executed judgment on the men that were joined to Baal-peor, and had stayed the plague from the congregation of Israel. He would be the minister of the Lord's vengeance on the wicked one, and it should be counted unto him for righteousness unto all generations for evermore.

He went down to the armoury in the Porter's lodge. Six pistols, he knew, were in the rack on the wall. Strange that tonight there were only five—a fresh proof of the justice of his fears. One of the five he selected, primed, loaded and cocked in readiness for the wizard's return. He took his stand in the shadow of the wall, at the entrance of the staircase. That his aim might be surer he left his candle burning at the stair-foot.

In solemn stillness the minutes drew themselves out into hours while Adoniram waited and prayed to himself. Then in the poring darkness he became sensible of a moving presence, noiseless and unseen. For a moment it appeared in the light of the candle, not two paces distant. It was the returning cat. A triumphant exclamation sprang to Byfield's lips, "God shall shoot at them, suddenly shall they be wounded"—and he fired.

With the report of the pistol there rang through the court a dismal outcry, not human nor animal, but resembling, as it seemed to the excited imagination of the chaplain, that of a lost soul in torment. With a scurry the creature disappeared in the darkness of the court, and Byfield did not pursue it. The deed was done— that he felt sure of—and as he replaced the pistol in the rack a gush of religious exaltation filled his heart. That night there was no return of the pattering steps outside his door, and he slept well.

* * *

Next day the body of Thomas Allen was discovered in the grove which girds the college—his breast pierced by a bullet. It was surmised that he had dragged himself thither from the court. There were tracks of blood from the staircase foot, where it was conjectured that he had shot himself, and a pistol was missing from the armoury. Some of the inmates of the court had been aroused by the discharge of the weapon. The general conclusion was that recorded by Sherman—that the fatal act was prompted by brooding melancholy.

Of his part in the night's transactions Byfield said nothing. The grim intelligence, succeeding the religious excitation of the night, brought to him questioning, dread, horror. Whatever others might surmise, he was fatally convinced that it was by his hand that Allen had died. Pity for the dead man had no place in the dark cabin of his soul. But how was it with himself? How should his action be weighed before the awful Throne? His lurid thought pictured the Great Judgment as already begun, the Book opened, the Accuser of the Brethren standing to resist him, and the dreadful sentence of Cain pronounced upon him, "Now art thou cursed from the earth."

In the evening he heard them bring the dead man to the chamber above his own. They laid him on his bed, and, closing the door, left him and descended the stairs. The sound of their footsteps died away and left a dreadful silence. As the darkness grew the horror of the stillness became insupportable. How he yearned that he might hear again the familiar muffled voice in the room above! And in an access of fervour he prayed aloud that the terrible present might pass from him, that the hours might go back, as on the dial of Ahaz, and all might be as yesterday.

Suddenly, as the prayer died on his lips, the silence was broken. He could not be mistaken. Very quietly he heard Allen's door open, and the old, pattering steps crept softly down the stairs. They passed his door. They were gone before he could rise from his knees to open it. A momentary flash lighted the gloom in Byfield's soul. What if his prayer was heard, if Allen was not dead, if the events of the past twenty-four hours were only a dream and a delusion of the Wicked One? Then the horror returned intensified. Allen was assuredly dead. This creeping Thing— what might it be?

For an hour in his room Byfield sat in agonised dread. Most the thought of the open door possessed him like a nightmare. Somehow it must be closed before the foul Thing returned. Somehow the mangled shape within must be barred up from the wicked powers that might possess it. The fancy gripped and stuck to his delirious mind. It was horrible, but it must be done. In a cold terror he opened his door and looked out.

A flickering light played on the landing above. Byfield hesitated. But the thought that the cat might return at any moment gave him a desperate courage. He mounted the stairs to Allen's door. Precisely as yesternight it stood wide open. Inside the room the books, the instruments, the magical figures were unchanged, and a candle, exposed to the night wind from the casement, threw wavering shadows on the walls and floor. At a glance he saw it all, and he saw the bed where, a few hours ago, the poor remains of Allen had been laid. The coverlet lay smooth upon it. The dead necromancer was not there.

Then as he stood foot-bound, at the door a wandering breath from the window caught the taper, and with a gasp the flame went out. In the black silence he became conscious of a moving sound. Nearer, up the stairs, they drew—the soft creeping steps—and in panic he shrank backwards into Allen's room before their advance. Already they were on the last flight of the stairs; and then in the doorway the darkness parted and Byfield saw. In a ring of pallid light that seemed to emanate from its body he beheld the cat—horrible, gory, its foreparts hanging in ragged collops from its neck. Slowly it crept into the room, and its eyes, smoking with dull malevolence, were fastened on Byfield. Further he backed into the room, to the corner where the bed was laid. The creature followed. It crouched to spring upon him. He dropped in a sitting posture on the bed and as he saw it launch itself upon him, he closed his eyes and found speech in a gush of prayer, "O my God, make haste for my help." In an agony he collapsed upon the couch and clutched its covering with both hands. Beneath it he gripped the stiffened limbs of the dead necromancer, and, when he opened his eyes, the darkness had returned and the spectral cat was gone.

THE GREATER FESTIVAL OF MASKS

Thomas Ligotti

I'll repeat what I said in my introduction to *Songs of a Dead Dreamer*, the first collection of Thomas Ligotti's tales: I don't know when I have enjoyed a collection of an author's horror stories more. That book was published in an edition of three hundred copies. I hope I am not the only editor to set about rescuing Ligotti—one of the most original writers in the field today—from such obscurity. I'm not in awe of many contemporary horror writers, but I am of Ligotti.

THERE ARE ONLY a few houses here but enough to make a street, many narrow streets, a town. The missing faces are not missed, not by Noss or anyone else, for they were never there to begin with and will not be there at the end. In the slender gaps and larger empty spaces between those houses stretching high or spreading low, which Noss observes, there was nothing at the beginning and will be nothing at the end. However, these imaginary houses, the ones now absent, may at some point change places with those which can be seen, in order to enrich the lapses in the landscape and give the visible a rest within nullity. Or perhaps for no reason at all, or none conceivable. For these are the declining days of the festival when the beginning and the end, the old and the new, the existent and the nonexistent all join in the masquerades.

But even at this stage of the festival some have yet to take a large enough interest in tradition to visit one of the shops of costumes and masks. Until recently Noss was among this group, for reasons neither he nor anyone else could clearly explain. Now, however, he is on his way to a shop on the edge of town whose every shelf is crammed and flowing over, even at this late stage of the festival, with costumes and masks. In the course of his wandering, or what seems like wandering through both the main and marginal sections of the town, Noss vaguely takes note of numerous indications of the festival season. These signs are sometimes subtle, sometimes blatant in nature. For instance, a few windows are unobtrusively left unshuttered, even throughout the day, and dim lights are left burning in empty rooms throughout the night. On the other hand, someone has ostentatiously made the effort to leave in the street a bunch of filthy rags splotched with various dyes; these rags are easily disturbed by the wind which howls constantly through the town, and they twist gaily about. There are other items, both deliberate and inadvertent, among the debris of festive abandonment: a hat, all style mangled out of it, has gotten stuck where a board is missing in a high fence, and it is thus relieved of having to perform a cripple's dance upon the windy street; upon a brown wall a poster has been diagonally peeled away, leaving a half-face almost wholly splashed into anonymity by dark rain and perhaps a little pale wine; and into strange pathways of caprice revelers will go, but to have *shorn* themselves in doorways, to have littered the shadows with such wiry clippings and tumbling fluff. Reliquiae of the hatless, the faceless, the tediously groomed. And Noss passes it all by with no more, if no less, than a glance.

His attention appears more sharply awakened as he approaches the center of the town, where the houses, the shops, the fences, the walls are more, much more . . . close. There seems barely enough space for a few stars to squeeze their bristling light between the roofs and towers above, and the outsized moon—not a familiar face in this neighborhood—must suffer to be seen only as a fuzzy anonymous glow mirrored in silvery windows. The streets are more tightly strung here, and a single one may have several names compressed into it from end to end. Some of the names have arisen not from community planning, or even from the quirks of civic history, as much as they seem to be due to an inexplicable need for the superfluous, as if a street sloughed off its name every so often like an old skin, the extra ones insuring that it would not go completely nameless. Perhaps a similar need, in this district, could account for the seemingly pointless embellishments common in its building: false doors which are elaborately decorated and also unopenable; massive shutters with blank walls behind them; enticing balconies, well railed and promising in their views, but without any means of entrance; stairways that enter dark niches . . . and a dead end. These structural adornments are mysterious indulgences in an area so pressed for room that even shadows must be shared. And so must other things. Backyards, for example, where a few fires still burn, the last of the festival pyres. For in this part of town the season is still in full swing, or at least the signs of its termination have yet to appear. Perhaps revelers hereabouts are still nudging each other in corners, proposing the ridiculous, coughing in the middle of jokes, asking favors. Here the festival is not dead. For the dominant rule is that activity does not radiate out from the center of the town, but seeps inward from its margins. The festival itself may have begun in some isolated shack on the city limits, if not in some even more remote residence in the woods beyond. In any case, its agitations have now reached the heart, and Noss is finally to visit one of the many shops of costumes and masks.

A little stairway puts him on a little platform of a porch, and a little slot of a door puts him inside the shop. The brief aforementioned description of the shop, and the abundance of its stock in trade, was not misleading. It is echoed here for emphasis: the shelves *are* crammed and flowing over with costumes and masks. The shelves are also very dark and mouthlike, stuffed into silence by the wardrobes and faces of dreams. Noss pulls at a mask that is overhanging the edge of a shelf—a dozen fall down upon him. Backing away from the avalanche of false faces, he looks at the sardonically grinning one in his hand.

"Excellent choice," says the shopkeeper, who steps out from behind a long counter in the rearguard of shadows. "Put it on and let's see. Yes, you see, this is excellent. You see how your entire face is well covered, from the hairline to just beneath the chin and no farther. And at the sides it clings snugly. It doesn't pinch, am I right?" The mask nods in agreement. "Good, that's how it should be. Your ears are unobstructed—you have very nice ones, by the way—while the mask clings snugly to the sides of the head. It is comfortable, yet secure enough to stay put and not fall off in the heat of activity. You'll see, after a while you won't even know you're wearing it! The holes for the eyes, nostrils, and mouth are perfectly placed for your features; no natural function is inhibited, that is a must. And it looks so good on you, especially up close, though I'm sure also at a distance. Go stand over there in the moonlight. Yes, it was made for you, what do you say? I'm sorry, what?"

Noss walks back toward the shopkeeper and removes the mask.

"I said all right, I suppose I'll take this one."

"Fine, there's no question about it. Now let me show you some of the other ones, just a few steps this way."

The shopkeeper pulls something down from a high shelf and places it in Noss's hands. What Noss now holds is another mask, but one that somehow seems to be . . . impractical. While the other mask possessed every virtue of conformity with its wearer's face, this mask is neglectful or unconcerned with such advantages. Its surface forms a strange mass of bulges and depressions which appear unaccommodating at best, possibly pain inflicting. And it is so much heavier than the first one.

"No," says Noss, handing back the mask. "I believe the other will do."

The shopkeeper looks as if he is at a loss for words. He stares at Noss for many moments before saying: "May I ask a personal question? Have you lived all your life . . . here?"

The shopkeeper's gesture beyond the thick

glass of the shop's windows provides the reference for "here."

Noss shakes his head in reply.

"Well, then there's no rush. Don't make any hasty decisions, hang around the shop and think it over, there's still time. In fact, it would be a favor to me. I have to go out for a while, you see, and if you could stay here and keep an eye on things I would greatly appreciate it. You'll do it, then? Good. And don't worry," he says, taking a large hat from a peg upon the wall, "I'll be back in no time, no time at all. And if someone pays us a visit, just do what you can for them," he shouts before closing the front door behind him.

Now alone, Noss takes a little better look at the masks the shopkeeper had earlier shown him. While differing in design, as any good assortment of masks must, they all share the same impracticalities of weight and shape, as well as having some very oddly placed apertures for ventilation, and too many of them. Noss gives these new masks back to the shelves from which they come, and he holds on tightly to the one which the shopkeeper had said was so perfect for him, so practical in every way. After a vaguely exploratory shuffle about the floor, Noss finds a stool behind the long counter and there falls asleep.

It seems only a few moments later that he is

awakened by some sound or other. Collecting his wits, he gazes around the dark shop, as if searching for the source of hidden voices which are calling to him. Then the sound returns, a soft thudding sound behind him and far off into the darkened rear rooms of the shop. Leaving the stool, Noss passes through a narrow doorway, descends a brief flight of stairs, passes through another doorway, ascends another brief flight of stairs, walks down a short and very low hallway to arrive at the back door of the shop. It thuds again once or twice. "If someone pays us a visit, just do what you can for them," Noss repeats to himself in a sleepy voice. But he looks uneasy. There is only a tiny plot of backyard on the other side of that door, surrounded by high fences. How did anyone get in, and why?

"Why don't you come around the front?" he shouts through the solid door.

After a pause, the reply comes: "Please bring five of the masks to the other side of the fence, that's where we are now. There's a fire, you'll see us. Well, will you do it or not?"

Noss leans his head into the shadows upon the wall: one side of his face is now in darkness and the other side is only semidistinct, blurred by a strange glare which is to real light what transitory drafts are to a true wind.

"Give me a moment," he calls through the door. "I'll meet you there. Did you hear me?"

There is no response from the other side. Noss turns the door handle, which is unexpectedly warm, and through a threadlike crack peers out into the dark yard. There is nothing to be seen except a square of blackness surrounded by the tall wooden slabs of the fence, and a few thin branches twist against a pale sky. But whatever signs of pranksterism Noss perceives or is able to fabricate to himself, there is no defying one's participation in festival activities, even if one can claim to have merely adopted this town and its seasonal practices, however *rare* they may be. For innocence and excuses are not harmonious with the spirit of this fabulously infrequent era, not in the least. Therefore, Noss retrieves the masks and goes out into the yard with them.

When he reaches the far end of the yard—a much greater distance from the shop than it had seemed to be—he sees a faint glow of fire through the cracks in the fence. There is a small door with clumsy black hinges and only a hole for a handle. Setting the five masks aside for a moment, Noss squats down to look through the hole with one eye. On the other side of the fence is a dark yard exactly like the one he is in, save for the fire burning upon the ground. Gathered around the blaze are several figures—five, perhaps four—with hunched shoulders and spines curving toward the light of the flames. At first the masks seem secure upon their faces; but one by one they appear to loosen and slip down, as if each is losing hold upon its wearer. Finally, one of the figures pulls his off completely and tosses it into the fire, where it curls and shrinks into a wad of bubbling blackness. The others follow this action when their time comes. Relieved of their masks, the figures resume their shrugging stance. But the light of the fire now shines on four, yes four, smooth and faceless faces.

"These are the wrong ones, you little idiot," says someone in the shadows next to Noss, who watches as a hand snatches up the masks and draws them into the darkness. "We have no more use for *these!*" the voice shouts.

And before Noss runs in retreat toward the shop, the five masks striking his narrow back and falling faceup upon the ground, he has a glimpse of the speaker in the shadows and acquires a rough idea why *those* masks are no good to them now.

Once again inside the shop, Noss leans upon the long counter to catch his breath. Then he looks up and sees that the shopkeeper has returned.

"There were some masks I brought out to the fence. They were the wrong ones," he says to the shopkeeper.

"No trouble at all," the other replies. "I'll see that the right ones get to them. Don't worry, there's still time. And how about you, then?"

"Me?"

"And the masks, I mean."

"Oh, I'm sorry to have bothered you in the first place. It's not at all what I thought it would be. Maybe I should never have come here. Maybe I should go back—"

"Nonsense! You can't leave now, you see. Let me take care of everything. Listen to me, I want you to go to a place where they know how to handle cases like this, at times like this. You're not the only one who is a little frightened tonight. It's right around the corner this, no that way, and across the street. It's a tall gray building, but it hasn't been there very long so watch you don't miss it. And you have to go down some stairs around the side. Now will you please follow my advice?"

Noss nods obediently.

"Good, you won't be sorry. Now go straight there. Don't stop for anyone or anything. And here, don't forget these," the shopkeeper reminds Noss, handing him an unmatching pair of masks. "Good luck!"

Though there doesn't seem to be anyone or anything to stop for, Noss does stop once or twice and dead in his tracks, as if someone behind him has just called his name. Then he thoughtfully caresses his chin and his smooth cheeks; he also touches other parts of his face, frantically, before proceeding toward the tall gray building. By the time he reaches the stairway at the side of the building, he cannot keep his hands off himself. Finally he puts on one of the masks—the sardonically grinning one, the one that once fit him so well. But now it appears to fit not quite as well. It keeps slipping, little by little, as Noss descends the stairs, which look worn down by countless footsteps and bowed in the middle by the invisible tonnage of time. But didn't the shopkeeper say this place hadn't been here very long?

The room at the bottom, where Noss now enters, also looks very old, and it is very . . . quiet. At this late stage of the festival the room is crowded with occupants who do nothing but sit silently in the shadows, with a face here and there reflecting the dull light. These faces are horribly simple; they have no expression to speak of, or very slight expressions and ones that are strange. But they are finding their way back, little by little, to a familiar land of faces. And the process, if the ear listens closely, is not an entirely silent one. Perhaps this is how a garden would sound if it could be heard growing in the dead of night. It is that soft creaking of new faces breaking through old flesh. The new faces are growing nicely. How happy Noss must be to have brought along a new mask for his new face. That wise old shopkeeper! He removes the old mask and tosses it to the ground, where it lands visage-up. In the dim glow it grins with an expression that later many will find strange and wonder at.

For the old festival of masks has ended, so that a greater festival may begin. And of the old time nothing will be said, because there was never anything to say; and nothing will be recalled, because there was never anything to recall. But the old masks, false souls, will find something to remember, and perhaps they will speak of those days when they are alone behind closed doors that do not open, or in the darkness at the summit of stairways leading nowhere.

THE WAR IS OVER

David Case

An anecdote. The Fifth World Fantasy Convention was held in Providence in 1979, in the Biltmore Plaza, and at lunchtime on Saturday I found myself in the bar. I eventually noticed that I was being gazed at by a man in a fisherman's cap. His wife heard my accent, and being English herself, came over to ask me why we were all wearing name badges. Her husband was a writer who had come into Providence that morning to rent a replacement for his electric typewriter. He wrote horror stories, and his name was David Case. He'd come in for a drink, quite unaware that the hotel was full of people who admired such fine books of his as *Fengriffen* and *The Cell*. I know of stranger coincidences, but not many. Later books include *Wolf Tracks* and *The Third Grave*. Before you read on, it is only fair to warn you that his work has lost none of its power.

MARIA SCHELL WAS humming happily to herself as she strolled past the shattered cathedral and turned into the narrow side street. The cathedral wall was down, spilling across the footpath, but the bell tower still stood, rooted in rubble but rising towards heaven. Maria had to step through broken bricks but she scarcely noticed. She was used to such things and the ruined buildings no longer troubled her. The war was over and the rebuilding had begun. The zoo had reopened that morning. Maria was happy today, much happier than she had been in a long time. In her hand she clutched the key to the apartment Rudolf had taken when he de-

cided to stay in the city. She had been clutching
it all during her walk, afraid to entrust it to a
pocket. It was more than a key to her, it was a
symbol. It was heavy and solid and durable,
linked to a heavy chain, and she held it as if it
were a talisman guiding her through the dam-
aged streets. Rudolf was staying and Maria knew
he was staying because of her . . . her and Katya.
He was staying and she was happy.

She went lightly up the steps and into the
shadowed hallway. She was a bit early but she
didn't mind waiting and, with the key, she could
let herself in. She swung the key. A figure moved
and she saw that a man was standing before
Rudolf's door, one hand raised but motionless,
as if he had just knocked and was waiting for a
response. He turned as she approached. He was
wearing a uniform . . . the hated uniform of the
enemy. But Maria didn't falter. The war was
over, Rudolf had taught her that, and she managed a smile as she walked up to him.

"Are you looking for Rudolf?"

He was a tall man, and handsome; it pleased
her that she was able to see that one of the
enemy was handsome, that they were not all
dark brutes.

He nodded.

"He isn't home at the moment. But he
should be back in an hour or so. You are . . . a
friend?"

She couldn't help looking at his uniform.

"We were in the war together," he said, speaking the language well. "I thought to call on him. I am Paul."

"And I am Maria. A . . . friend. He has spoken of me?"

"I have not seen him in some time."

Maria hesitated, then smiled and said, "I have a key. If you would care to wait with me?"

"That would be convenient."

Maria used the key, fumbling a bit with the strange lock. It turned with a clunk. The soldier followed her into the pleasant room. A skylight blocked an oblong of pale daylight in the center of the floor and from a tall, arched window a narrow shaft reached out towards the oblong, like ethereal spirits seeking to make contact in the vast reaches of space. The corners of the room were dark. Maria had only been there once before, but she felt quite comfortable playing the hostess to Rudolf's friend. She offered him a chair and sat opposite, then immediately jumped up again.

"Will you take coffee?"

"I will."

She went into the small kitchen. She was still holding the key in her hand. It clanked against the coffee pot and she laughed. She put it in her pocket where its weight dragged reassuringly at her hip. It was pleasant, entertaining here, just as if she were Rudolf's wife. She brought the coffee in on a lacquered tray, real coffee, too, not the wartime stuff. She poured. Paul held his cup and saucer rather awkwardly on his knee.

"Is Rudolf . . . well?"

"Oh yes. Very well."

The man looked faintly surprised.

"He is happy?"

"I . . . believe so."

"I am pleased. Sometimes war . . ." He shrugged. He was really a very handsome man and he moved well, except for his awkwardness with the coffee cup.

"My husband, too, was a soldier," she said. "He is dead."

"The war?"

"Yes."

He nodded, looking at her. "And now you are the friend of Rudolf . . ." he said.

"Yes, the war has ended."

"But grief remains."

Her eyes flickered over his uniform again. She wondered if he resented her. She said, "At first, of course, I hated you all. The very sight of the uniform you wear would have caused me pain. But I think differently now, Rudolf has taught me different."

"You are very fond of him, then?"

Maria lowered her eyes demurely, a pretty

woman who blushed gracefully and was not ashamed. "I am fond of him, yes. I believe he is fond of me."

"I am surprised. Pleased, but surprised."

"At my forgiveness?"

"At Rudolf's forgiveness. Surprised and . . . satisfied. I must tell you, I worried for my friend. That is why I journeyed here to see him. It was not easy for him."

"He never speaks of it."

"No, he was never a man to talk abundantly."

"More coffee?"

She moved lightly, not embarrassed by her body.

"I can see why he is fond of you," Paul said, but his smile was a compliment, his words no insult.

"He should be home soon," Maria said. Then she leaned closer to the man and added, "He came to me shortly after the armistice, you see. You must not think me one to consort with the enemy"—she smiled at the word—"but for extraordinary circumstances. He travelled here to find me, for my husband, although a soldier of the other side, had died in his arms. My husband had been reported missing and presumed dead, but I did not know, and hope can be a terrible thing, a desperate thing. It was thoughtful and kind of Rudolf, to call upon the widow of a fallen foe . . . to assure me that my husband had died bravely and that his last words, his last thoughts, had been of me . . . of his wife and child. That is a thing to keep, a thing better than false hope. That was some weeks ago. We have since become friendly. Katya . . . my daughter . . . adores Rudolf. Even while I still saw him, despite his kindness, as an enemy soldier . . . well, they say a child can always tell when a person is kind, and good . . ."

"They say that, yes."

"He is very good with children, Rudolf. See, here is a photograph we took in the park . . . that is my little Katya, with Rudolf . . . see how she laughs?"

"A handsome child."

"She is just five."

Maria put the photograph in the pocket with the key.

"Yes. Rudolf's daughter would have been about that age. He was devoted to the child, to children. I knew him rather well."

Maria's face clouded.

"His daughter died in the war," she said. "He told me that. His wife and daughter. A tragic thing. The bombing, I suppose?"

"He hasn't told you?"

"As you say, he talks little."

"Not the bombing."

"Oh?" she said, but Paul was looking down into his coffee cup, swirling the dark fluid. He

seemed to be searching for something submerged there, or reflected.

Maria said, "That, perhaps, was why he felt
compelled to visit me, to lessen my loss in
any way he could. A loss we had shared. It was
natural that we became friends. My daughter . . . " She looked up with a sudden boldness.
"She needs a father."

"Ah . . ."

"Has he . . . written you?"

"He has not. But that would not be in his
nature, if he felt an . . . emotion . . ." he ges-
tured vaguely.

"This is shameless of me," she said. "I should
not question you, forgive me. It's just that I wish
to know him better, to know his thoughts. I am
confused within my mind. Perhaps I love him."
Her hands moved before her, toward him. "The
memory of my husband suspends itself above my
feelings, clouding them. But I am young. Is it
wrong of me to love again?" She looked away,
toward the tall, arched window. "To wed?"

"Not wrong. But has Rudolf spoken of this?"

"Not in words. Sometimes, in his eyes, when
he gazes at me . . . I sense a longing. A tor-
mented longing . . . But I must not talk this
way . . ."

"Not at all. I am his friend, I am pleased he is
no longer bitter. You may confide in me."

"The war is over and it is wrong for either side

to bear malice, he has taught me that by his gentleness. Both sides were wicked, at times . . . not perhaps as wicked as the propaganda made out. I admire Rudolf's tolerance, his quiet, sorrowful tolerance. He has known pain, yet he has renounced hatred, not by words but by his nature. And I like to believe I have helped him, too. I have tried . . . I am willing to try, if he so wishes . . ." She broke off, uncertain, half smiling, then said, "Our zoo has reopened today. Many of the animals were killed, but it has reopened. There is a tiger. Rudolf has taken Katya to the zoo. They wished to go alone . . . a good sign, I think. I think perhaps today he will make a decision, that he wished to be apart from me while he makes that decision. Afterwards I shall prepare dinner here in his apartment. Perhaps you will stay? I should like that, Paul. Am I rambling? I am nervous and happy . . . we have not spoken of the future, of a future together, but often I feel he is thinking of it, planning for it. He knows, I believe, that I am willing."

"It would be good for Rudolf to wed again."

Maria looked at him gratefully.

"I believed him dangerously close to . . . imbalance."

Her eyes widened. "Rudolf? Oh, no."

"After his wife and child were killed, you understand."

"Ah."

"Enough for any man . . ."

"He never speaks of that. The war . . . was he very brave? I am sure he was very brave."

"He was a good soldier."

"I should wish to hear of his past, his life . . . to know him more completely."

Paul was silent.

"His wife and child . . . you say it was not the bombing?"

"Not the bombing, no."

"Will you tell me?"

"It was . . . painful."

Maria shuddered with the sympathetic vibration of shared pain.

"Tell me of it," she said.

"It is not my place to speak. If he wishes you to know . . . or not to know . . ."

"I would share his pain."

Paul looked down into his cup again, peering into the liquid as if looking for a sign in the entrails of a sheep. A tic moved at the corner of his mouth. The decision was there in the cup. Then he straightened and raised the cup, drained it. The decision was still there, it was in his belly now. He looked at Maria and she knew he was going to tell her; it was registered in his troubled eyes.

He began to speak slowly, seeking out the words.

"It was near the end of the fighting and the

enemy . . . and your soldiers had been scattered, the ranks broken, many wandering alone or in small bands behind the lines. All was confusion. We—Rudolf and I—were jubilant. It was soon to end and we wished to fight no more. We had become separated from our company, a thing we did not try hard to avoid, and we were near to Rudolf's home, his cabin in the forest. He had sent his wife and child to live in the cabin, months before, to avoid the bombing in the city—before the tide had turned. He blames himself for that decision, that terrible decision . . . but at the time . . . Well, we took it into our minds that it would be good to go to that cabin and peacefully wait for the armistice; to take advantage of the confusion and kill no more. We set off through the valley. The walk would be no more than half a day, and although Rudolf was eager to see his family we did not hurry . . . he was savouring the expectation. And then we came upon an enemy soldier. We broke through some undergrowth and there he was, face-to-face with us. He was armed, as were we. We regarded one another. He was lost and frightened. We walked on, passing him without a word; I believe Rudolf nodded to him. It made us feel good to pass him by in peace. But then Rudolf began to think. If the scattered soldiers were this far behind the lines, they might well have come upon the cabin. Beaten men, tired, sick, desperate. We hastened, then. We arrived only minutes too late."

Paul paused. He peered at Maria like a lecturer gauging his audience and the pause disturbed her. It seemed unnecessarily dramatic and artificial, done for effect.

"Please go on," she said.

"That, in many ways, is the worst part, that he arrived only moments too late to save them but just in time to see the results with the bodies still warm . . ."

Maria felt her spine tingle and a terrible chill passed through her flesh, numbing her. Paul regarded her calmly and for a moment she thought he had finished, that he had told her enough. She had heard enough. She regretted asking him to tell her. Then he continued.

"It was one of the soldiers, of course. He was still there. Rudolf's wife had been raped and strangled. His daughter, a child of four, had been bayonetted . . . disemboweled before her mother's eyes. For no reason, no reason at all. An act of war," he said, bitterly.

"My God!" Maria was trembling.

"You can see . . ."

"That one of our soldiers would do such a thing . . . that any man . . ." Her hands dragged down her cheeks, distorting her countenance. Her eyes seemed unnaturally large. "And that Rudolf can still forgive, that he could come to

263

me, console me, when his own terrible grief . . .
that he can look kindly upon us when most men
would scream for revenge . . ."

"He took revenge."

She stared at him, her eyes red. The angles of
light were shifting across the floor, stretching
out towards one another but not yet linking their
pale illumination. The room no longer seemed
pleasant, the shadows were deeper at the edges.

Paul's tongue ran across his lips.

He said, "We took the man. He was naked and
smeared with blood and we took him living. He
seemed stunned by his own actions and offered
no resistance. He was quite calm, really. He
said, 'I don't know what came over me, why I
would have done such a thing,' just as if he were
apologizing for some minor oversight. He kept
shaking his head from side to side. 'No,' he said,
'this was not like me, I regret this.' His amazing
attitude calmed Rudolf. Rudolf seemed . . . less
than human . . . a block of living ice, his emo-
tions frozen to preserve his sanity. He knelt
beside the bodies, he did not touch them. He
looked at them, his face terrible in its lack of
expression, its absolute lack of expression. Then
he regarded the man. And then . . . but you will
not wish to hear this . . ."

Maria said nothing for she did not wish to hear
more.

And Paul said, "He was not, then, the kind man you know him to be."

"But how could he be . . . then . . . that fiend . . ."

"Rudolf tortured him," Paul said, abruptly.

Maria winced. She realized that Paul was going to continue . . . that the pause had been as before, for effect. She wanted to tell him to stop, to tell him she could bear no more, but he had begun again, speaking softly and holding her fixed with his steady gaze.

"He commenced, in the most calculating manner, to torture the man to death. I wished to stop him. I could not. His dead wife and child were there and I could not bring myself to intervene. I could not even depart. Sickened, I was yet fascinated. I watched. For two days and two nights, there in the pleasant rustic cabin, he tortured the man. I made to bury his wife and child; he prevented this. The bodies remained with us. He would pause from time to time, weary from his efforts, and gaze at the bodies, breathing deeply . . . as if drawing in the strength to continue. And then he would return to his task. I slept. I woke. He was still inflicting unspeakable pain, with steel and fire . . . to this day my slumber churns with nightmares . . ."

"I cannot believe . . . yet if you were there . . . if you are telling the truth, if in his uncontrollable agony . . . that terrible man deserved it and . . ." She faltered.

Paul was waiting, watching her. He seemed to be interested in her reactions . . . interested in the effect his words had had. "That man . . . ," he said.

"Enough!"

"I cannot pity him, yet I had to admire him. I have never known such bravery . . ."

"I have heard enough, Paul . . ."

"Through all his unspeakable torment, the man refused to cry out, to beg for mercy . . ."

Maria's eyes widened.

"Paul! You came here to tell me this!" she whispered, her voice taut, vibrant with strained chords.

"But you asked me, my dear . . ."

"You came to tell me!"

He held up his hand, palm towards her.

"There is little more," he said and, incredibly, he seemed to be smiling. He leaned forward in his chair, only an inch or two and yet his face seemed to rush towards her. Maria drew back, cringing.

"The man knew he was going to die, perhaps knew he was deserving of such a death . . . such a hideous death. He was resigned to it. It was only a matter of time and you could tell that he was waiting it out. Patiently. That is the word, patiently. Waiting for the pain to end . . . waiting for death as one waits for a train . . . patiently, annoyed at the delay but knowing that, eventually, it will come.

"And that, of course, made it worse for Rudolf."

Paul looked at his watch as if he, too, were waiting for something to come.

"Rudolf could take no satisfaction from the man's agony . . . it made his own agony worse. And then he saw a different way. Thinking of his own terrible loss, he saw a method, a vengeance to fit the crime. The man's identity papers were there, in his discarded uniform. Rudolf took them out and looked at them. He smiled, nodding to himself. He returned to the man and held the papers before his face. The man looked at them. He had only one eye left by this time, but with that solitary eye he looked at the papers and then he turned that eye upwards and looked into Rudolf's smiling face. He knew! There was no need to explain it to him, it was manifested in Rudolf's smile . . . a smile such as I had never seen before, nor wish to see again . . . a smile of infinite satisfaction.

"The brave soldier was not then so brave. He pleaded, he begged. He called upon God. Soon he could no longer plead with words, for he had no tongue, but his solitary eye continued to beg and the thick blood bubbling from his lips seemed a runic plea. A shudder passed through him. His whole form vibrated. Rudolf did not want him to die so soon. Rudolf lifted his ruined face, he held the man's head in his arms with a strange tenderness. A thick drop of blood ran sluggishly down from the man's empty eye socket. It fascinated Rudolf, he watched it advance down the man's face. It reached his jaw, it hung suspended there for a moment. When it dropped free, the man was dead.

"He had died in Rudolf's arms . . ."

Maria thought that she was screaming, but there was no sound. She screamed in silence. The light from the tall window reached the greater light from the skylight. The illumination joined. A bell sounded from somewhere in the city and Paul looked at his watch. Paul shrugged.

"Well, you see, the man was dead and could no longer feel pain and Rudolf was alive and his terrible agony remained. For a time I feared for his sanity. But from what you tell me, he seems to have recovered now and I am pleased . . . pleased that he has forgotten his plan for further vengeance, even befriending the widow of a fallen foe. It is a good sign. I am Rudolf's friend. I have known him long. I would do anything for him. But, my dear . . . You have gone so white! You are spilling your coffee. Now what is the matter with you?"

UPON THE DULL EARTH

EARTH

Philip K. Dick

How many of Philip K. Dick's stories are tales of terror? In my experience, quite a few, but perhaps that matters less than the eloquence of his best writing, among which I would include his vision of Tagore, the second coming of Christ. Whether or not it was objectively real, I find it heartbreaking. His great theme was the nature of reality, even here in one of his earliest and strangest stories, a tale of terror if ever he wrote one.

SILVIA RAN LAUGHING through the night brightness, between the roses and cosmos and Shasta daisies, down the gravel paths, and beyond the heaps of sweet-tasting grass swept from the lawns. Stars, caught in pools of water, glittered everywhere, as she brushed through them to the slope beyond the brick wall. Cedars supported the sky and ignored the slim shape squeezing past, her brown hair flying, her eyes flashing.

"Wait for me," Rick complained, as he cautiously threaded his way after her, along the half-familiar path. Silvia danced on without stopping. "Slow down!" he shouted angrily.

"Can't—we're late." Without warning, Silvia

appeared in front of him, blocking the path. "Empty your pockets," she gasped, her grey eyes sparkling. "Throw away all metal. You know they can't stand metal."

Rick searched his pockets. In his overcoat were two dimes and a fifty-cent piece. "Do these count?"

"*Yes!*" Silvia snatched the coins and threw them into the dark heaps of calla lilies. The bits of metal hissed into the moist depths and were gone. "Anything else?" She caught hold of his arm anxiously. "They're already on their way. Anything else, Rick?"

"Just my watch." Rick pulled his wrist away as Silvia's wild fingers snatched for the watch. "*That's* not going in the bushes."

"Then lay it on the sundial—or the wall. Or in a hollow tree." Silvia raced off again. "Throw away your cigarette case. And your keys, your belt buckle—everything metal. You know how they hate metal. Hurry, we're late!"

Rick followed sullenly after her. "All right, *witch*."

Silvia snapped at him furiously from the darkness. "Don't *say* that. It isn't true. You've been listening to my sisters and my mother and—"

Her words were drowned out by the sound. Distant flapping, a long way off, like vast leaves rustling in a winter storm. The night sky was alive with the frantic poundings; they were coming very quickly this time. They were too greedy, too desperately eager to wait. Flickers of fear touched the man and he ran to catch up with Silvia.

Silvia was a tiny column of green skirt and blouse in the centre of the thrashing mass. She was pushing them away with one arm and trying to manage the faucet with the other. The churning activity of wings and bodies twisted her like a reed. For a time she was lost from sight.

"Rick!" she called faintly. "Come here and help!" She pushed them away and struggled up. "They're suffocating me!"

Rick fought his way through the wall of flashing white to the edge of the trough. They were drinking greedily at the blood that spilled from the wooden faucet. He pulled Silvia close against him; she was terrified and trembling. He held her tight until some of the violence and fury around them had died down.

"They're hungry," Silvia gasped feebly.

"You're a little cretin for coming ahead. They can sear you to ash!"

"I know. They can do anything." She shuddered, excited and frightened. "Look at them," she whispered, her voice husky with awe. "Look at the size of them—their wingspread. And they're *white*, Rick. Spotless—perfect. There's nothing in our world as spotless as that. Great and clean and wonderful."

"They certainly wanted the lamb's blood."

Silvia's soft hair blew against his face as the wings fluttered on all sides. They were leaving now, roaring up into the sky. Not up, really— away. Back to their own world, whence they had scented the blood. But it was not only the blood—they had come because of Silvia. *She* had attracted them.

The girl's grey eyes were wide. She reached up towards the rising white creatures. One of them swooped close. Grass and flowers sizzled as blinding white flames roared in a brief fountain. Rick scrambled away. The flaming figure hovered momentarily over Silvia and then there was a hollow *pop*. The last of the white-winged giants was gone. The air, the ground, gradually cooled into darkness and silence.

"I'm sorry," Silvia whispered.

"Don't do it again," Rick managed. He was numb with shock. "It isn't safe."

"Sometimes I forget. I'm sorry, Rick. I didn't mean to draw them so close." She tried to smile. "I haven't been that careless in months. Not since that other time when I first brought you out here." The avid, wild look slid across her face. "Did you *see* him? Power and flames! And he didn't even touch us. He just—looked at us. That was all. And everything's burned up, all around."

Rick grabbed hold of her. "Listen," he grated. "You mustn't call them again. It's wrong. This isn't their world."

"It's not wrong—it's beautiful."

"It's not safe!" His fingers dug into her flesh until she gasped. "Stop tempting them down here!"

Silvia laughed hysterically. She pulled away from him, out into the blasted circle that the horde of angels had seared behind them as they rose into the sky. "I can't *help* it," she cried. "I belong with them. They're my family, my people. Generations of them, back into the past."

"What do you mean?"

"They're my ancestors. And someday I'll join them."

"You're a little witch!" Rick shouted furiously.

"No," Silvia answered. "Not a witch, Rick. Don't you see? I'm a saint."

The kitchen was warm and bright. Silvia plugged in the Silex and got a big red can of coffee down from the cupboards over the sink. "You mustn't listen to them," she said, as she set out plates and cups and got cream from the refrigerator. "You know they don't understand. Look at them in there."

Silvia's mother and her sisters, Betty Lou and Jean, stood huddled together in the living room, fearful and alert, watching the young couple in the kitchen. Walter Everett was standing by the fireplace, his face blank, remote.

"Listen to *me*," Rick said. "You have this power to attract them. You mean you're not—isn't Walter your real father?"

"Oh, yes—of course he is. I'm completely human. Don't I look human?"

"But you're the only one who has the power."

"I'm not physically different," Silvia said thoughtfully. "I have the ability to see, that's all. Others have had it before me—saints, martyrs. When I was a child, my mother read to me about St. Bernadette. Remember where her cave was? Near a hospital. They were hovering there and she saw one of them."

"But the blood! It's grotesque. There never was anything like that."

"Oh, yes. The blood draws them, lamb's blood especially. They hover over battlefields. Valkyries—carrying off the dead to Valhalla. That's why saints and martyrs cut and mutilate themselves. You know where I got the idea?"

Silvia fastened a little apron around her waist and filled the Silex with coffee. "When I was nine years old, I read of it in Homer, in the Odyssey. Ulysses dug a trench in the ground and filled it with blood to attract the spirits. The shades from the nether world."

"That's right," Rick admitted reluctantly. "I remember."

"The ghosts of people who died. They had lived once. Everybody lives here, then dies and goes there." Her face glowed. "We're all going to have wings. We're all going to fly. We'll be filled with fire and power. We won't be worms any more."

"Worms! That's what you always call me."

"Of course you're a worm. We're all worms—grubby worms creeping over the crust of the Earth, through dust and dirt."

"Why should blood bring them?"

"Because it's life and they're attracted by life. Blood is *uisge beatha*—the water of life."

"Blood means death! A trough of spilled blood . . ."

"It's *not* death. When you see a caterpillar crawl into its cocoon, do you think it's dying?"

Walter Everett was standing in the doorway. He stood listening to his daughter, his face dark. "One day," he said hoarsely, "they're going to grab her and carry her off. She wants to go with them. She's waiting for that day."

"You see?" Silvia said to Rick. "He doesn't understand either." She shut off the Silex and poured coffee. "Coffee for you?" she asked her father.

"No," Everett said.

277

"Silvia," Rick said, as if speaking to a child, "if you went away with them, you know you couldn't come back to us."

"We all have to cross sooner or later. It's all part of our life."

"But you're only nineteen," Rick pleaded. "You're young and healthy and beautiful. And our marriage—what about the marriage?" He half rose from the table. "Silvia, you've got to stop this!"

"I *can't* stop it. I was seven when I saw them first." Silvia stood by the sink, gripping the Silex, a faraway look in her eyes. "Remember, Daddy? We were living back in Chicago. It was winter. I fell, walking home from school." She held up a slim arm. "See the scar? I fell and cut myself on the gravel and slush. I came home crying—it was sleeting and the wind was howling around me. My arm was bleeding and my mitten was soaked with blood. And then I looked up and saw them."

There was silence.

"They want you," Everett said wretchedly. "They're flies—bluebottles, hovering around, waiting for you. Calling you to come along with them."

"Why not?" Silvia's grey eyes were shining and her cheeks radiated joy and anticipation. "You've seen them, Daddy. You know what it means. Transfiguration—from clay into gods!"

Rick left the kitchen. In the living room the two sisters stood together, curious and uneasy. Mrs. Everett stood by herself, her face granite-hard, eyes bleak behind her steel-rimmed glasses. She turned away as Rick passed them.

"What happened out there?" Betty Lou asked him in a taut whisper. She was fifteen, skinny and plain, hollow cheeked, with mousy, sand-coloured hair. "Silvia never lets us come out with her."

"Nothing happened," Rick answered.

Anger stirred the girl's barren face. "That's not true. You were both out in the garden, in the dark, and—"

"Don't talk to him!" her mother snapped. She yanked the two girls away and shot Rick a glare of hatred and misery. Then she turned quickly from him.

Rick opened the door to the basement and switched on the light. He descended slowly into the cold, damp room of concrete and dirt, with its unwinking yellow light hanging from dust-covered wires overhead.

In one corner loomed the big floor furnace with its mammoth hot air pipes. Beside it stood the water heater and discarded bundles, boxes of books, newspapers, and old furniture, thick with dust, encrusted with strings of spider webs.

At the far end were the washing machine and

spin dryer. And Silvia's pump and refrigeration system.

From the work bench Rick selected a hammer and two heavy pipe wrenches. He was moving towards the elaborate tanks and pipes when Silvia appeared abruptly at the top of the stairs, her coffee cup in one hand.

She hurried quickly down to him. "What are you doing down here?" she asked, studying him intently. "Why that hammer and those two wrenches?"

Rick dropped the tools back on to the bench. "I thought maybe this could be solved on the spot."

Silvia moved between him and the tanks. "I thought you understood. They've always been a part of my life. When I brought you with me the first time, you seemed to see what—"

"I don't want to lose you," Rick said harshly, "to anybody or anything—in this world or any other. *I'm not going to give you up.*"

"It's not giving me up!" Her eyes narrowed. "You came down here to destroy and break everything. The moment I'm not looking you'll smash all this, won't you?"

"That's right."

Fear replaced anger on the girl's face. "Do you want me to be chained here? I have to go on—I'm through with this part of the journey. I've stayed here long enough."

"Can't you wait?" Rick demanded furiously. He couldn't keep the ragged edge of despair out of his voice. "Doesn't it come soon enough anyhow?"

Silvia shrugged and turned away, her arms folded, her red lips tight together. "You want to be a worm always. A fuzzy, little creeping caterpillar."

"I want *you*."

"You can't *have* me!" She whirled angrily. "I don't have any time to waste with this."

"You have higher things in mind," Rick said savagely.

"Of course." She softened a little. "I'm sorry, Rick. Remember Icarus? You want to fly, too. I know it."

"In my time."

"Why not now? Why wait? You're afraid." She slid lightly away from him, cunning twisting her red lips. "Rick, I want to show you something. Promise me first—you won't tell anybody."

"What is it?"

"Promise?" She put her hand to his mouth. "I have to be careful. It cost a lot of money. Nobody knows about it. It's what they do in China—everything goes towards it."

"I'm curious," Rick said. Uneasiness flicked at him. "Show it to me."

Trembling with excitement, Silvia disappeared behind the huge lumbering refrigerator, back into the darkness behind the web of frost-hard freezing coils. He could hear her tugging and pulling at something. Scraping sounds, sounds of something large being dragged out.

"See?" Silvia gasped. "Give me a hand, Rick. It's heavy. Hardwood and brass—and metal lined. It's hand stained and polished. And that carving—see the carving! Isn't it beautiful?"

"What is it?" Rick demanded huskily.

"It's my cocoon," Silvia said simply. She settled down in a contented heap on the floor, and rested her head happily against the polished oak coffin.

Rick grabbed her by the arm and dragged her to her feet. "You can't sit with that coffin, down here in the basement with—" He broke off. "What's the matter?"

Silvia's face was twisting with pain. She backed away from him and put her finger quickly to her mouth. "I cut myself—when you pulled me up—on a nail or something." A thin trickle of blood oozed down her fingers. She groped in her pocket for a handkerchief.

"Let me see it." He moved towards her, but she avoided him. "Is it bad?" he demanded.

"Stay away from me," Silvia whispered.

"What's wrong? Let me see it!"

"Rick," Silvia said in a low intense voice, "get some water and adhesive tape. As quickly as possible." She was trying to keep down her rising terror. "I have to stop the bleeding."

"Upstairs?" He moved awkwardly away. "It doesn't look too bad. Why don't you . . ."

"Hurry." The girl's voice was suddenly bleak with fear. "Rick, *hurry!*"

Confused, he ran a few steps.

Silvia's terror poured after him. "No, it's too late," she called thinly. "Don't come back—keep away from me. It's my own fault. I trained them to come. *Keep away! I'm sorry, Rick. Oh*—" Her voice was lost to him, as the wall of the basement burst and shattered. A cloud of luminous white forced its way through and blazed out into the basement.

It was Silvia they were after. She ran a few hesitant steps towards Rick, halted uncertainly, then the white mass of bodies and wings settled around her. She shrieked once. Then a violent explosion blasted the basement into a shimmering dance of furnace heat.

He was thrown to the floor. The cement was hot and dry—the whole basement crackled with heat. Windows shattered as pulsing white shapes pushed out again. Smoke and flames licked up the walls. The ceiling sagged and rained plaster down.

Rick struggled to his feet. The furious activity was dying away. The basement was a littered chaos. All surfaces were scorched black, seared, and crusted with smoking ash. Splintered wood, torn cloth, and broken concrete were strewn everywhere. The furnace and washing machine were in ruins. The elaborate pumping and refrigeration system—now a glittering mass of slag. One whole wall had been twisted aside. Plaster was rubbed over everything.

Silvia was a twisted heap, arms and legs doubled grotesquely. Shrivelled, carbonized remains of fire-scorched ash, settling in a vague mound. What had been left behind were charred fragments, a brittle burned-out husk.

It was a dark night, cold and intense. A few stars glittered like ice from above his head. A faint, dank wind stirred through the dripping calla lilies and whipped gravel up in a frigid mist along the path between the black roses.

He crouched for a long time, listening and watching. Behind the cedars, the big house loomed against the sky. At the bottom of the slope a few cars slithered along the highway. Otherwise, there was no sound. Ahead of him jutted the squat outline of the porcelain trough and the pipe that had carried blood from the refrigerator in the basement. The trough was empty and dry, except for a few leaves that had fallen in it.

Rick took a deep breath of thin night air and

held it. Then he got stiffly to his feet. He scanned the sky, but saw no movement. They were there, though, watching and waiting—dim shadows, echoing into the legendary past, a line of god-figures.

He picked up the heavy gallon drums, dragged them to the trough and poured blood from a New Jersey abattoir, cheap-grade steer refuse, thick and clotted. It splashed against his clothes and he backed away nervously. But nothing stirred in the air above. The garden was silent, drenched with night fog and darkness.

He stood beside the trough, waiting and wondering if they were coming. They had come for Silvia, not merely for the blood. Without her there was no attraction but the raw food. He carried the empty metal cans over to the bushes and kicked them down the slope. He searched his pockets carefully, to make sure there was no metal on him.

Over the years, Silvia had nourished their habit of coming. Now she was on the other side. Did that mean they wouldn't come? Somewhere in the damp bushes something rustled. An animal or a bird?

In the trough the blood glistened, heavy and dull, like old lead. It was their time to come, but nothing stirred the great trees above. He picked out the rows of nodding black roses, the gravel path down which he and Silvia had run—

violently he shut out the recent memory of her flashing eyes and deep red lips. The highway beyond the slope—the empty, deserted garden —the silent house in which her family huddled and waited. After a time, there was a dull, swishing sound. He tensed, but it was only a diesel truck lumbering along the highway, headlights blazing.

He stood grimly, his feet apart, his heels dug into the soft black ground. He wasn't leaving. He was staying there until they came. He wanted her back—at any cost.

Overhead, foggy webs of moisture drifted across the moon. The sky was a vast barren plain, without life or warmth. The deathly cold of deep space, away from suns and living things. He gazed up until his neck ached. Cold stars, sliding in and out of the matted layer of fog. Was there anything else? Didn't they want to come, or weren't they interested in him? It had been Silvia who had interested them—now they had her.

Behind him there was a movement without sound. He sensed it and started to turn, but suddenly, on all sides, the trees and undergrowth shifted. Like cardboard props they wavered and ran together, blending dully in the night shadows. Something moved through them, rapidly, silently, then was gone.

They had come. He could feel them. They had

shut off their power and flame. Cold, indifferent statues, rising among the trees, dwarfing the cedars—remote from him and his world, attracted by curiosity and mild habit.

"Silvia," he said. "Which are you?"

There was no response. Perhaps she wasn't among them. He felt foolish. A vague flicker of white drifted past the trough, hovered momentarily and then went on without stopping. The air above the trough vibrated, then died into immobility, as another giant inspected briefly and withdrew.

Panic breathed through him. They were leaving again, receding back into their own world. The trough had been rejected; they weren't interested.

"Wait," he muttered thickly.

Some of the white shadows lingered. He approached them slowly, wary of their flickering immensity. If one of them touched him, he would sizzle briefly and puff into a dark heap of ash. A few feet away he halted.

"You know what I want," he said. "I want her back. She shouldn't have been taken yet."

Silence.

"You were too greedy," he said. "You did the wrong thing. She was going to come over to you, eventually. She had it all worked out."

The dark fog rustled. Among the trees the flickering shapes stirred and pulsed responsive to his voice. "*True*," came a detached, impersonal sound. The sound drifted around him, from tree to tree, without location or direction. It was swept off by the night wind to die into dim echoes.

Relief settled over him. They had passed—they were aware of him—listening to what he had to say.

"You think it's right?" he demanded. "She had a long life here. We were going to marry, have children."

There was no answer. But he was conscious of a growing tension. He listened intently, but he couldn't make out anything. Presently he realized a struggle was taking place, a conflict among them. The tension grew—more shapes flickered—the clouds, the icy stars, were obscured by the vast presence, swelling around him.

"Rick!" A voice spoke close by. Wavering, drifting back into the dim regions of the trees and dripping plants. He could hardly bear it—the words were gone as soon as they were spoken. "Rick—help me get back."

"Where are you?" He couldn't locate her. "What can I do?"

"I don't know." Her voice was wild with bewilderment and pain. "I don't understand. Something went wrong. They must have thought I—wanted to come right away. I *didn't!*"

"I know," Rick said. "It was an accident."

"They were waiting. The cocoon, the trough —but it was too soon." Her terror came across to him, from the vague distances of another universe. "Rick, I've changed my mind. I want to come back."

"It's not as simple as that."

"I know. Rick, time is different on this side. I've been gone so long—your world seems to creep along. It's been years, hasn't it?"

"One week," Rick said.

"It was their fault. You don't blame me, do you? They know they did the wrong thing. Those who did it have been punished, but that doesn't help me." Misery and panic distorted her voice so he could hardly understand her. "How can I come back?"

"Don't they know?"

"They say it can't be done." Her voice trembled. "They say they destroyed the clay part—it was incinerated. There's nothing for me to go back to."

Rick took a deep breath. "Make them find some other way. It's up to them. Don't they have the power? They took you over too soon—they must send you back. It's *their* responsibility."

The white shapes shifted uneasily. The conflict rose sharply; they couldn't agree. Rick warily moved back a few paces.

"They say it's dangerous." Silvia's voice came

from no particular spot. "They say it was attempted once." She tried to control her voice. "The nexus between this world and yours is unstable. There are vast amounts of free-floating energy. The power we—on this side—have isn't really our own. It's a universal energy, tapped and controlled."

"Why can't they . . ."

"This is a higher continuum. There's a natural process of energy from lower to higher regions. But the reverse process is risky. The blood—it's a sort of guide to follow—a bright marker."

"Like moths around a light bulb," Rick said bitterly.

"If they send me back and something went wrong—" She broke off and then continued, "If they make a mistake, I might be lost between the two regions. I might be absorbed by the free energy. It seems to be partly alive. It's not understood. Remember Prometheus and the fire . . ."

"I see," Rick said, as calmly as he could.

"Darling, if they try to send me back, I'll have to find some shape to enter. You see, I don't exactly have a shape any more. There's no real material form on this side. What you see, the wings and the whiteness, are not really there. If I succeeded in making the trip back to your side . . ."

"You'd have to mould something," Rick said.

"I'd have to take something there—something of clay. I'd have to enter it and reshape it. As He did a long time ago, when the original form was put on your world."

"If they did it once, they can do it again."

"The One who did that is gone. He passed on upward." There was unhappy irony in her voice. "There are regions beyond this. The ladder doesn't stop here. Nobody knows where it ends, it just seems to keep on going up and up. World after world."

"Who decides about you?" Rick demanded.

"It's up to me," Silvia said faintly. "They say, if I want to take the chance, they'll try it."

"What do you think you'll do?" he asked.

"I'm afraid. What if something goes wrong? You haven't seen it, the region between. The possibilities there are incredible—they terrify me. He was the only one with enough courage. Everyone else has been afraid."

"It was their fault. They have to take responsibility."

"They know that." Silvia hesitated miserably. "Rick, darling, please tell me what to do."

"Come back!"

Silence. Then her voice, thin and pathetic. "All right, Rick. If you think that's the right thing."

"It is," he said firmly. He forced his mind not to think, not to picture or imagine anything. *He*

291

had to have her back. "Tell them to get started now. Tell them—"

A deafening crack of heat burst in front of him. He was lifted up and tossed into a flaming sea of pure energy. They were leaving and the scalding lake of sheer power bellowed and thundered around him. For a split second he thought he glimpsed Silvia, her hands reaching imploringly towards him.

Then the fire cooled and he lay blinded in dripping, night-moistened darkness. Alone in the silence.

Walter Everett was helping him up. "You damn fool!" he was saying, again and again. "You shouldn't have brought them back. They've got enough from us."

Then he was in the big, warm living room. Mrs. Everett stood silently in front of him, her face hard and expressionless. The two daughters hovered anxiously around him, fluttering and curious, eyes wide with morbid fascination.

"I'll be all right," Rick muttered. His clothing was charred and blackened. He rubbed black ash from his face. Bits of dried grass stuck to his hair—they had seared a circle around him as they'd ascended. He lay back against the couch and closed his eyes. When he opened them, Betty Lou Everett was forcing a glass of water into his hand.

"Thanks," he muttered.

"You should never have gone out there," Walter Everett repeated. "Why? Why'd you do it? You know what happened to her. You want the same thing to happen to you?"

"I want her back," Rick said quietly.

"Are you mad? You can't get her back. She's gone." His lips twitched convulsively. "You saw her."

Betty Lou was gazing at Rick intently. "What happened out there?" she demanded. "They came again, didn't they?"

Rick got heavily to his feet and left the living room. In the kitchen he emptied the water in the sink and poured himself a drink. While he was leaning wearily against the sink, Betty Lou appeared in the doorway.

"What do you want?" Rick demanded.

The girl's thin face was flushed an unhealthy red. "I know something happened out there. You were feeding them, weren't you?" She advanced towards him. "You're trying to get her back?"

"That's right," Rick said.

Betty Lou giggled nervously. "But you can't. She's dead—her body's been cremated—I saw it." Her face worked excitedly. "Daddy always said that something bad would happen to her, and it did." She leaned close to Rick. "She was a witch! She got what she deserved!"

"She's coming back," Rick said.

"*No!*" Panic stirred the girl's drab features. "She *can't* come back. She's dead—like she always said—worm into butterfly—she's a butterfly!"

"Go inside," Rick said.

"You can't order me around," Betty Lou answered. Her voice rose hysterically. "This is *my* house. We don't want you around here any more. Daddy's going to tell you. He doesn't want you and I don't want you and my mother and sister . . ."

The change came without warning. Like a film gone dead. Betty Lou froze, her mouth half open, one arm raised, her words dead on her tongue. She was suspended, an instantly lifeless thing raised slightly off the floor, as if caught between two slides of glass. A vacant insect, without speech or sound, inert and hollow. Not dead, but abruptly thinned back to primordial inanimacy.

Into the captured shell filtered new potency and being. It settled over her, a rainbow of life that poured into place eagerly—like hot fluid—into every part of her. The girl stumbled and moaned; her body jerked violently and pitched against the wall. A china teacup tumbled from an overhead shelf and smashed on the floor. The girl retreated numbly, one hand to her mouth, her eyes wide with pain and shock.

"Oh!" she gasped. "I cut myself." She shook her head and gazed up mutely at him, appealing to him. "On a nail or something."

"*Silvia!*" He caught hold of her and dragged her to her feet, away from the wall. It was *her* arm he gripped, warm and full and mature. Stunned grey eyes, brown hair, quivering breasts—she was now as she had been those last moments in the basement.

"Let's see it," he said. He tore her hand from her mouth and shakily examined her finger. There was no cut, only a thin white line rapidly dimming. "It's all right, honey. You're all right. There's nothing wrong with you!"

"Rick, I was over *there*." Her voice was husky and faint. "They came and dragged me across with them." She shuddered violently. "Rick, am I actually *back*?"

He crushed her tight. "Completely back."

"It was so long. I was over there a century. Endless ages. I thought—" Suddenly she pulled away. "Rick . . ."

"What is it?"

Silvia's face was wild with fear. "There's something wrong."

"There's nothing wrong. You've come back home and that's all that matters."

Silvia retreated from him. "But they took a living form, didn't they? Not discarded clay.

They don't have the power, Rick. They altered His work instead." Her voice rose in panic. "A mistake—they should have known better than to alter the balance. It's unstable and none of them can control the . . ."

Rick blocked the doorway. "Stop talking like that!" he said fiercely. "It's worth it—*anything's* worth it. If they set things out of balance, it's their own fault."

"We can't turn it back!" Her voice rose shrilly, thin and hard, like drawn wire. "We've set it in motion, started the waves lapping out. The balance He set up is *altered*."

"Come on, darling," Rick said. "Let's go and sit in the living room with your family. You'll feel better. You'll have to try to recover from this."

They approached the three seated figures, two on the couch, one in the straight chair by the fireplace. The figures sat motionless, their faces blank, their bodies limp and waxen, dulled forms that did not respond as the couple entered the room.

Rick halted, uncomprehending. Walter Everett was slumped forward, newspaper in one hand, slippers on his feet; his pipe was still smoking in the deep ashtray on the arm of his chair. Mrs. Everett sat with a lapful of sewing, her face grim and stern, but strangely vague. An unformed face, as if the material were melting and running together. Jean sat huddled in a shapeless heap, a ball of clay wadded up, more formless each moment.

Abruptly Jean collapsed. Her arms fell loose beside her. Her head sagged. Her body, her arms, and legs filled out. Her features altered rapidly. Her clothing changed. Colours flowed in her hair, her eyes, her skin. The waxen pallor was gone.

Pressing her finger to her lips she gazed up at Rick mutely. She blinked and her eyes focused. "Oh," she gasped. Her lips moved awkwardly; the voice was faint and uneven, like a poor soundtrack. She struggled up jerkily, with unco-ordinated movements that propelled her stiffly to her feet and towards him—one awkward step at a time—like a wire dummy.

"Rick, I cut myself," she said. "On a nail or something."

What had been Mrs. Everett stirred. Shapeless and vague, it made dull sounds and flopped grotesquely. Gradually it hardened and shaped itself. "My finger," its voice gasped feebly. Like mirror echoes dimming off into darkness, the third figure in the easy chair took up the words. Soon, they were all of them repeating the phrase, four fingers, their lips moving in unison.

"My finger. I cut myself, Rick."

Parrot reflections, receding mimicries of words and movement. And the settling shapes were familiar in every detail. Again and again, repeated around him, twice on the couch, in the easy chair, close beside him—so close he could hear her breathe and see her trembling lips.

"What is it?" the Silvia beside him asked.

On the couch one Silvia resumed its sewing—she was sewing methodically, absorbed in her work. In the deep chair another took up its newspapers, its pipe and continued reading. One huddled, nervous and afraid. The one beside him followed as he retreated to the door. She was panting with uncertainty, her grey eyes wide, her nostrils flaring.

"Rick . . ."

He pulled the door open and made his way out on to the dark porch. Machinelike, he felt his way down the steps, through the pools of night collected everywhere, towards the driveway. In the yellow square of light behind him, Silvia was outlined, peering unhappily after him. And behind her, the other figures, identical, pure repetitions, nodding over their tasks.

He found his coupé and pulled out on to the road.

Gloomy trees and houses flashed past. He wondered how far it would go. Lapping waves spreading out—a widening circle as the imbalance spread.

He turned on to the main highway; there were soon more cars around him. He tried to see into them, but they moved too swiftly. The car ahead was a red Plymouth. A heavyset man in a blue business suit was driving, laughing merrily with the woman beside him. He pulled his own coupé up close behind the Plymouth and followed it. The man flashed gold teeth, grinned, waved his plump hands. The girl was dark haired, pretty. She smiled at the man, adjusted her white gloves, smoothed down her hair, then rolled up the window on her side.

He lost the Plymouth. A heavy diesel truck cut in between them. Desperately he swerved around the truck and nosed in beyond the swift-moving red sedan. Presently it passed him and, for a moment, the two occupants were clearly framed. The girl resembled Silvia. The same delicate line of her small chin—the same deep lips, parting slightly when she smiled—the same slender arms and hands. It was Silvia. The Plymouth turned off and there was no other car ahead of him.

He drove for hours through the heavy night darkness. The gas gauge dropped lower and lower. Ahead of him dismal rolling countryside spread out, blank fields between towns and unwinking stars suspended in the bleak sky. Once, a cluster of red and yellow lights gleamed. An intersection—filling stations and a big neon sign. He drove on past it.

At a single-pump stand, he pulled the car off the highway, on to the oil-soaked gravel. He climbed out, his shoes crunching the stone underfoot, as he grabbed the gas hose and unscrewed the cap of his car's tank. He had the tank almost full when the door of the drab station building opened and a slim woman in white overalls and navy shirt, with a little cap lost in her brown curls, stepped out.

"Good evening, Rick," she said quietly.

He put back the gas hose. Then he was driving out on to the highway. Had he screwed the cap on again? He didn't remember. He gained speed. He had gone over a hundred miles. He was nearing the state line.

At a little roadside café, warm, yellow light glowed in the chill gloom of early morning. He slowed the car down and parked at the edge of the highway in the deserted parking lot. Bleary-eyed he pushed the door open and entered.

Hot, thick smells of cooking ham and black coffee surrounded him, the comfortable sight of people eating; a jukebox blared in the corner. He threw himself on to a stool and hunched over, his head in his hands. A thin farmer next to him glanced at him curiously and then returned to his newspaper. Two hard-faced women across from him gazed at him momentarily. A handsome youth in denim jacket and jeans was eating red beans and rice, washing it down with steaming coffee from a heavy mug.

"What'll it be?" the pert blonde waitress

asked, a pencil behind her ear, her hair tied back in a tight bun. "Looks like you've got some hangover, mister."

He ordered coffee and vegetable soup. Soon he was eating, his hands working automatically. He found himself devouring a ham and cheese sandwich; had he ordered it? The jukebox blared and people came and went. There was a little town sprawled beside the road, set back in some gradual hills. Grey sunlight, cold and sterile, filtered down as morning came. He ate hot apple pie and sat wiping dully at his mouth with a paper napkin.

The café was silent. Outside nothing stirred. An uneasy calm hung over everything. The jukebox had ceased. None of the people at the counter stirred or spoke. An occasional truck roared past, damp and lumbering, windows rolled up tight.

When he looked up, Silvia was standing in front of him. Her arms were folded and she gazed vacantly past him. A bright yellow pencil was behind her ear. Her brown hair was tied back in a hard bun. At the counter others were sitting, other Silvias, dishes in front of them, half dozing or eating, some of them reading. Each the same as the next, except for their clothing.

He made his way back to his parked car. In half an hour he had crossed the state line. Cold, bright sunlight sparkled off dew-moist roofs and pavements as he sped through tiny unfamiliar towns.

Along the shiny morning streets he saw them moving—early risers, on their way to work. In twos and threes they walked, their heels echoing in sharp silence. At bus stops he saw groups of them collected together. In the houses, rising from their beds, eating breakfast, bathing, dressing, were more of them—hundreds of them, legions without number. A town of them preparing for the day, resuming their regular tasks, as the circle widened and spread.

He left the town behind. The car slowed under him as his foot slid heavily from the gas pedal. Two of them walked across a level field together. They carried books—children on their way to school. Repetitions, unvarying and identical. A dog circled excitedly after them, unconcerned, his joy untainted.

He drove on. Ahead a city loomed, its stern columns of office buildings sharply outlined against the sky. The streets swarmed with noise and activity as he passed through the main business section. Somewhere, near the centre of the city, he overtook the expanding periphery of the circle and emerged beyond. Diversity took the place of the endless figures of Silvia. Grey eyes and brown hair gave way to countless varieties of men and women, children and adults, of all ages and appearances. He increased his speed and raced out on the far side, on to the wide four-lane highway.

He finally slowed down. He was exhausted. He had driven for hours; his body was shaking with fatigue.

Ahead of him a carrot-haired youth was cheerfully thumbing a ride, a thin bean-pole in brown slacks and light camel's-hair sweater. Rick pulled to a halt and opened the front door. "Hop in," he said.

"Thanks, buddy." The youth hurried to the car and climbed in as Rick gathered speed. He slammed the door and settled gratefully back against the seat. "It was getting hot, standing there."

"How far are you going?" Rick demanded.

"All the way to Chicago." The youth grinned shyly. "Of course, I don't expect you to drive me that far. Anything at all is appreciated." He eyed Rick curiously. "Which way you going?"

"Anywhere," Rick said. "I'll drive you to Chicago."

"It's two hundred miles!"

"Fine," Rick said. He steered over into the left lane and gained speed. "If you want to go to New York, I'll drive you there."

"You feel all right?" The youth moved away uneasily. "I sure appreciate a lift, but . . ." He hesitated. "I mean, I don't want to take you out of your way."

Rick concentrated on the road ahead, his hands gripping hard around the rim of the wheel. "I'm going fast. I'm not slowing down or stopping."

"You better be careful," the youth warned in a troubled voice. "I don't want to get in an accident."

"I'll do the worrying."

"But it's dangerous. What if something happens? It's too risky."

"You're wrong," Rick muttered grimly, eyes on the road. "It's worth the risk."

"But if something goes wrong—" The voice broke off uncertainly and then continued, "I might be lost. It would be so easy. It's all so unstable." The voice trembled with worry and fear. "Rick, please . . ."

Rick whirled. "How do you know my name?"

The youth was crouched in a heap against the door. His face had a soft, molten look, as if it were losing its shape and sliding together in an unformed mass. "I want to come back," he was saying, from within himself, "but I'm afraid. You haven't seen it—the region between. It's nothing but energy, Rick. He tapped it a long time ago, but nobody else knows how."

The voice lightened, became clear and treble. The hair faded to a rich brown. Grey, frightened eyes flickered up at Rick. Hands frozen, he hunched over the wheel and forced himself not to move. Gradually he decreased speed and brought the car over into the right-hand lane.

"Are we stopping?" the shape beside him asked. It was Silvia's voice now. Like a new insect, drying in the sun, the shape hardened and locked into firm reality. Silvia struggled up on the seat and peered out. "Where are we? We're between towns."

He jammed on the brakes, reached past her and threw open the door. "Get out!"

Silvia gazed at him uncomprehendingly. "What do you mean?" she faltered. "Rick, what is it? What's wrong?"

"*Get out!*"

"Rick, I don't understand." She slid over a little. Her toes touched the pavement. "Is there something wrong with the car? I thought everything was all right."

He gently shoved her out and slammed the door. The car leaped ahead, out into the stream of mid-morning traffic. Behind him the small, dazed figure was pulling itself up, bewildered and injured. He forced his eyes from the rearview mirror and crushed down the gas pedal with all his weight.

The radio buzzed and clicked in vague static when he snapped it briefly on. He turned the dial and, after a time, a big network station came in. A faint, puzzled voice, a woman's voice. For a time he couldn't make out the words. Then he recognized it and, with a pang of panic, switched the thing off.

Her voice. Murmuring plaintively. Where was the station? Chicago. The circle had already spread that far.

He slowed down. There was no point hurrying. It had already passed him by and gone on. Kansas farms—sagging stores in little old Mississippi towns—along the bleak streets of New England manufacturing cities swarms of brown-haired grey-eyed women would be hurrying.

It would cross the ocean. Soon it would take in the whole world. Africa would be strange—kraals of white-skinned young women, all exactly alike, going about the primitive chores of hunting and fruit gathering, mashing grain, skinning animals. Building fires and weaving cloth and carefully shaping razor-sharp knives.

In China . . . he grinned inanely. She'd look strange there, too. In the austere high-collar suit, the almost monastic robe of the young Communist cadres. Parades marching up the main streets of Peiping. Row after row of slim-legged full-breasted girls, with heavy Russian-made rifles. Carrying spades, picks, shovels. Columns of cloth-booted soldiers. Fast-moving workers with their precious tools. Reviewed by an identical figure on the elaborate stand overlooking the street, one slender arm raised, her gentle, pretty face expressionless and wooden.

He turned off the highway on to a side road. A moment later he was on his way back, driving slowly, listlessly, the way he had come.

At an intersection a traffic cop waded out through traffic to his car. He sat rigid, hands on the wheel, waiting numbly.

"Rick," she whispered pleadingly as she reached the window. "Isn't everything all right?"

"Sure," he answered dully.

She reached in through the open window and touched him imploringly on the arm. Familiar fingers, red nails, the hand he knew so well. "I want to be with you so badly. Aren't we together again? Aren't I back?"

"Sure."

She shook her head miserably. "I don't understand," she repeated. "I thought it was all right again."

Savagely he put the car into motion and hurtled ahead. The intersection was left behind.

It was afternoon. He was exhausted, riddled with fatigue. He guided the car towards his own town automatically. Along the streets she hurried everywhere, on all sides. She was omnipresent. He came to his apartment building and parked.

The janitor greeted him in the empty hall. Rick identified him by the greasy rag clutched in one hand, the big push broom, the bucket of

307

wood shavings. "Please," she implored, "tell me what it is, Rick. Please tell me."

He pushed past her, but she caught at him desperately. "Rick, *I'm back*. Don't you understand? They took me too soon and then they sent me back again. It was a mistake. I won't ever call them again—that's all in the past." She followed after him, down the hall to the stairs. "I'm never going to call them again."

He climbed the stairs. Silvia hesitated, then settled down on the bottom step in a wretched, unhappy heap, a tiny figure in thick workman's clothing and huge cleated boots.

He unlocked his apartment door and entered.

The late afternoon sky was a deep blue beyond the windows. The roofs of nearby apartment buildings sparkled white in the sun.

His body ached. He wandered clumsily into the bathroom—it seemed alien and unfamiliar, a difficult place to find. He filled the bowl with hot water, rolled up his sleeves, and washed his face and hands in the swirling hot steam. Briefly, he glanced up.

It was a terrified reflection that showed out of the mirror above the bowl, a face, tearstained and frantic. The face was difficult to catch—it seemed to waver and slide. Grey eyes, bright with terror. Trembling red mouth, pulse-fluttering throat, soft brown hair. The face gazed

308

out pathetically—and then the girl at the bowl bent to dry herself.

She turned and moved wearily out of the bathroom into the living room.

Confused, she hesitated, then threw herself on to a chair and closed her eyes, sick with misery and fatigue.

"Rick," she murmured pleadingly. "Try to help me. I'm back, aren't I?" She shook her head, bewildered. "Please, Rick, I thought everything was all right."